Michael Krüger, a poet, novelist, and editor, was born in Wittgendorf, Germany in 1943. He has published three volumes of verse and won a number of literary awards, including the Peter Huchel Prize. Michael Krüger lives in Munich and is the editor of *Akzente*, one of the best-known literary magazines in Germany.

THE MAN in the TOWER

THE MAN in the TOWER

a novel

MICHAEL KRÜGER

Translated by Leslie Willson

GEORGE BRAZILLER

New York

First published in the United States of America in
1993 by George Braziller, Inc.

English translation copyright © 1992 by Leslie Willson
Originally published in German

Copyright © 1991 by Residenz Verlag under the title
Der Mann im Turm

Extracts from Laurence Binyon's translation of Dante's *Divine
Comedy* are reproduced by permission of Mrs. Nicolete Gray and
The Society of Authors on behalf of the Laurence Binyon Estate.

For information, write to the publisher:
George Braziller, Inc.
60 Madison Avenue
New York, NY 10010

Library of Congress Cataloging-in-Publication Data

Krüger, Michael, 1943-
 [Mann im Turm. English]
 The man in the tower : a novel / Michael Krüger.
 p.   cm.
 ISBN 0-8076-1297-9
 I. Title.
PT2671.R736M3613   1993
833'.914—dc20
                                      92-21534
                                      CIP

Printed in the United States of America
First U.S. edition

THE MAN in the TOWER

We went our separate ways.

In the log cabin I took the painting out of its frame, took the frame apart, and packed it in its box. Then I cut the canvas of the painting out of its stretcher, cut it into small pieces, and burned those pieces slowly in the stove. Then I took the stretcher apart and burned it, too. Then I burned all my sketches and finally the paints, the brushes, and the palette. What was left of my equipment, I set aside for later disposal. It did not surprise my neighbors, my landlords, that, in this summer night, smoke rose from my flue, for I had often had a fire in my stove during the past summer for my own purposes.

I now feel a freedom, a gladness, and a spaciousness in my heart as in a brightly illuminated universe.

—Adalbert Stifter

1

I was relieved to finally be in the tower again. A deep intactness emanated from objects, neither importunate nor guarded. For a long time I stood in the door, taking in that still life that was spread solemnly before me. All things, even the most ridiculous, find their way back to themselves when they are left alone for a while. The half-empty, un-corked bottle of red wine stood on the table, next to it the full ashtray, the cup, and a spatula on the top of the day-before-yesterday's newspaper. Next to that a brush, whose dry bristles pointed stiffly upward. Burnt, burnt-out sienna. A couple of loose clumps of paint had gotten onto the picture on the front page of the newspaper, which showed the pope in Santiago de Compostela. He had his eyes closed, and his folded hands touched the end of his nose. A remarkable holy man. Not his inconsiderate sense of truth, not the well-known choice of boundless possibilities, not the fear of perishing in the whirlpool of the world, rather some sort of petty, banal turn in his life had made him pope; otherwise he would have become a bus driver or the chief editor of Polish television. But one day his father stroked the shorn head of the boy and said, "Let yourself be consecrated as a priest, Karol; who knows what good might come of it." And the lad answered, first he had to finish his biology homework about the wedding dance of bees. Now he is the pope, and when he closes his eyes and touches his nose with folded hands, he gets onto the front page of all the newspapers in the civilized world.

As I pulled the wet clothes off my body and spread them over the back of a chair, I thought about which banal turn in my own life could have been responsible for my becoming a painter, and which other turn had brought me to this tower. The first question was difficult to answer, because all children draw, but the second one was easy. The tower belonged to the country estate of an art collector who bought my work; here in the southwest of France, he grew corn, sunflowers, and durum wheat. Once a month he came by train from Hamburg, walked across his fields, counted the kernels of corn on the cob, let the soil slide through his fingers, spoke with the manager, Monsieur Jopin, and then returned home. His presence transformed the estate for a week. Everyone listened to him, even the sunflowers, which suddenly stretched their heads agreeably and looked at him so that he could examine their seeds. He was the expert. In Hamburg he owned a large art collection, in which my pictures were represented. *Represented* is the correct word, for once when I visited him unannounced in Hamburg, they were not hanging on the walls.

He had turned the tower over to me for a year because I wanted to work on a grand series of pictures of the four seasons and needed a place where I could actually witness the changes in nature. He was to receive four watercolors as token compensation. I had been living in this tower now for four months, the harvest was in — the best in the region, of course — the new seed prepared, my friend had departed for the winter, which he would spend on a business trip in

South America, and except for the four watercolors, which without much reflection I had completed right after my arrival in order to relieve the pressure, I had hardly finished anything. Hundreds of color sketches and pencil drawings piled up in my studio, the highest room in the tower, but always, when I had set a canvas on the easel and arranged my brushes, something prevented me from getting to work. My hand refused and could not be persuaded, even by alcohol. Why does someone like me become a painter? I wandered around on the plowed fields for hours and, with my head bent, stared into the freshly dug furrows, in which the seed would soon be laid and from which the kernels would then sprout, the calculated transformation. But my canvas remained white. When I got the brush set, ready to impress the stamp of my familiarity with the sheer multiplicity of phenomena that lay outside my window, I capitulated before the palpable lack of intellectual order and wiped away what I wanted to depict. Everything was clear and flat, the incomparable beauty of my sketches could not be transferred to the canvas. When things got really bad and only a caustic, mean state of mind controlled me, I drove my car to the nearby town, sat in the café on the square, and drank pastis. The town was so small that everyone soon knew me; the café owner set a glass of pastis and a carafe of water before me without being asked. *Le Monde* and the *Herald Tribune* were laid on the counter for me in the news shop, and the owner of the dairy store, a man with a strongly expressive bulbous nose, went right to his noodle machine to make me an Italian pasta: tortellini stuffed with liver. I was at a high pitch and ready to be assailed by work. But it took its time. Obviously it did not yet think about making me its tool.

In order to stabilize my inner self, I read Dante's *Divine Comedy*. Perhaps with this indulgence I also wanted to meet head-on the lack of development of my own world view, which became most clear to me in my isolation. The power of experience, as Dante describes it, had been transmitted only very abstractly in my German postwar existence at a German secondary school; his spaces, which extend into infinity, were palpable only as a pale, shadowy echo in my fantasies. But the mysteriously impenetrable relationship that bound me to Dante's world, and that from my point of view might also be only the result of an immature confusion, this unequal but very grave relationship still kept me from surrendering to one of two immediate possibilities that were offered me after four months: merely to provide the pictures with color without becoming addicted to color and hawk them to the highest bidder — or to leave. I stayed, with Dante, the original first-person narrator.

Because I liked none of the translations I had brought along from Germany, I had begun trying one of my own, and my audacity went so far that I finally decided to offer an illustrated edition of my version. In the spring, when my friend returned from South America, I would ask him whether he could take over the financing of the project. He might even make some money from it, if special editions were produced with original drawings. I had more than enough.

So, in spite of the fact that my own work did not engage me, I was busy. It would also be wrong to characterize my condition as unhappy or aimless; I was restless, fidgety, but not really unhappy. Were not all great works preceded by an impatient vacuum? Why should fate treat me better? A small turn, just a tiny shift, and I would create something significant. Two days earlier, engaged by this precipitate certainty, I had sprung into my car with inexplicable excitement and driven to the town to be calmed down by the sight of people again.

2

On that afternoon the rue Gambetta was full of people, an unusual scene in this provincial town, in which ordinarily — except for some housewives with their net bags, several retired persons on the benches around the main square, and occasionally a group of Englishmen who, with their heads bent back and their Michelin guidebooks in hand, studied the Romanesque church — few people were to be found. That day I saw English, Dutch, and German cars in plenitude, and even the French ones rarely had "32", the identification number of our *département*, on their license plates. In the café the Dutchmen were drinking beer and pastis with their own boundless merriment, but still without displaying visible effects. So in the pale afternoon sun I was going to take a seat at one of the three plastic tables in front of the café, but all around them Englishmen were sprawled, drinking red wine, although they obviously had already drunk quite a lot of it. Only at the bar, with its four stools covered with red plush, was a place free.

Even before I perched on the worn-out monstrosity, my pastis was placed before me, next to it the water carafe, whose form and delicate colors I admired, and a small bowl of nuts that dissolved in the mouth and tasted like a wad of cotton. The café owner had a desperate expression, as though the unexpected increase in business was upsetting him, and he muttered incessantly to himself. One of the

Dutchmen walked time after time to the jukebox to select a Spanish song whose refrain the group then accompanied in a chorus while holding hands and laughing. Without this support, apparently, they would have fallen off their chairs or been embarrassed.

Hardly impressive, I thought, when I suddenly recognized myself again behind the bottles in the mirror: over a white, open collar, an expressionless face, suntanned, narrow, unshaven, that stared at me steadily as though I were seeing myself for the first time. Not exactly the face of a painter who was on the verge of adding a few more to the masterworks in museums. A mixture of cold, calculated certainty and desperate concentration, as though the gentleman with my face might be afraid of getting lost in his own emptiness. I suddenly remembered with what certainty I had entered the tower four months before, with what solemnity I had arranged the studio. A grayish blue storm front had crept from the south toward the tower and had delineated everything in the vicinity with such sharpness that, alarmed, I had to go outside. There, leaning against the gritty wall of the building, which was exhaling the warmth of the day, I riveted my glance onto the landscape that lay so far away, so silently, so unapproachably before me. Then the storm had passed, and the square around the building lay before me dull and inwardly turned — and I painted my first watercolor of that summer.

But what does a painter look like? I would also have imagined a Dante scholar differently, maybe with long, white hair, like the twentieth-century poet whose translation I consulted daily in spite of its foolish typeface. I tried a

16

couple of inconspicuous grimaces, pursed my lips, furrowed my brow, and let my cigarette hang nonchalantly to give my lame, uninteresting opposite some sort of style, and finally leaning my head to the side, I propped it up with my left hand and jerkily blew smoke through my nose. Of course, one can't look like anything if one wants to be a famous painter, I told myself; normality is plainly a requisite. Normal as hell! Still, in my situation I would not have minded if one of those drinkers, startled from his alcoholic stupor, had asked whether I wasn't the famous German painter whose name he had just forgotten, the guy with the burnt sienna, the driven one, the gloomy one? But the question remained unasked. Probably there were too many painters in the world, too many pictures that no one could or would look at anymore. Since every nut had become an art expert so he could invest his money correctly, paintings multiplied like mushrooms. The worst stuff was sold at auction. And even if the paintings were good, they couldn't help being bad, because everybody had forgotten how to see them; but, for all that, there were paintings on walls and in vaults.

I had sunk so deeply into a sudden torpidity that at first I did not notice the couple sitting next to me on the barstools, although both were speaking German to one another. Now, in the mirror, I saw the swollen, reddened face of the man, who was next to me, and beside it the gaunt face of the woman, both about my age. The man spoke freely, while with his thick hand he kept slapping the brass molding that ran along the bar as a grip for drinkers. The woman endured his talking without saying anything. She looked tired, wispy, somewhat embittered, anything but beautiful — rather even somewhat common, with her big, vindictive nose. Even so, I now stared at her unswervingly, without hearing the whispered babble of the fat man, which washed over the woman without ceasing.

The subject was money, responsibility, recklessness, and the phrase I heard most often, which sprang out of the flow of words, was *pay the price*. A German family fight, I thought; she wrecked the car, now they're stuck for good in this godforsaken place, and he has to pay the penalty for her recklessness. What didn't fit this picture was the appearance of the fat man. In his tailored suit with a vest, his half boots with purple socks, the purple pocket handkerchief, and the strange chain he wore over his shirt, on which something was dangling that I couldn't quite make out, he didn't look like a tourist who was interested in the Judgment Day on a tympanum. Blasé, smooth, worldly. Something or other between a used-car dealer and Metro-Goldwyn-Mayer, I thought, just as the woman opened her mouth for the first time.

"Peter," she said, slightly lengthening it, mouth open, mouth closed. "Peter."

Nothing more. Just simply: Peter. But her *Peter* sounded as though she firmly believed those two syllables would have an effect. Far from it, since the sole noticeable effect was a slight rise in Fat Peter's voice, as though he wanted to wipe away, talk down, erase, eliminate the obstacle of the two short syllables. And, in fact, soon thereafter he had fallen back into his old tone

18

of voice. Then the woman, sighing and shaking her head slightly, went to the ladies' room and for an eternity did not return.

I ordered a new pastis. Fat Peter had helped himself to my cigarettes out of nervousness and because he had to keep a rein on what he was saying, but he noticed his mistake immediately and begged my pardon in the best French. Not only that, he had now laid his own cigarette case more or less in front of my nose, where it lay unused, the matches on top of it. And finally, with the most obvious gesture, so as not to be obvious, he gave the café owner, who was pouring me another pastis, a quiet signal that he would take care of that drink: with the second of his thick fingers he drew a half circle several times. With that the matter was settled, done, and he shoved his thick rear end off the red barstool, and he, too, set out waddling to the toilet. I was imagining how he would manage the unwieldy French toilet in his suit, when the woman returned, pale and rumpled, hesitated for a moment as though she had the feeling that she had wound up in the wrong restaurant, and then again sat down on the stool. I would like to have sketched her then: her disconsolate weariness, the resigned way she held her cigarette, her dry cough, the erratic gesture with which she touched her hair. I looked at her from the side unabashedly; she watched me in the mirror. The Spanish song was still playing, and all the while the very drunken Dutchmen babbled blissfully along with the melody. What might her name be? Barbara? Ilse? Helga? Peter and Helga? An Arab in a floor-length caftan came shuffling from the back room, where incessantly squealing slot machines were set up. Behind him, with short steps, walked Fat Peter, neatly buttoned up and wagging his right arm excitedly, as though a decisive argument had occurred to him while squatting.

3

It was cold in the tower. Cold and clammy. My feet seemed to stick to the red, six-sided floor tiles, and they left behind footprints that were larger than their soles. Still in my underpants, I stacked wood in the fireplace and lighted it with the help of *Le Monde*. The pope in Purgatory, if that were at all possible. Thick smoke was now hanging in the kitchen, but I had no desire to open the window. Outside, it was still pouring in streams; the rain was falling to the earth evenly and vertically. When the fire was finally burning, I went up to the parlor, which was situated on the mezzanine between my studio and the kitchen and which served also as my bedroom because I had reserved the top floor entirely for my work. The bed was unmade, and the hide cover hung onto the floor. I put on dry pants and a pullover, and with *The Divine Comedy* went back down to the kitchen without having thrown even a glance at my studio. Autumn had to wait. I briefly imagined the gallery owner who wanted to visit me after Christmas to prepare for the exhibition at the end of March, complete with catalogue.

"We'll take pictures of you and your tower," he had said, "like a photograph by Wols — a romantic backdrop for grand opera. Finally, painting sets out again for the countryside, into solitude, to cast a last look at true nature before the ultimate concrete cover."

My God! If he only knew what it looked like here.

Fields, fields everywhere, gentle hills and small patches of woods from which the bare branches of the sickly elms reared into the gray sky. If the EC kept supporting the farmers, in fifty years it would look the same here. And the romantic tower in the solitude had running hot water, electric lights, and a telephone.

She had only to call, but she did not do so.

She let me dangle. I picked up the telephone receiver to see whether it was working, but put it right down again so that it would not be busy if she called. But she did not want to disturb me at all.

So, then, Dante. I had long ago given up translating it entirely, rather looked for a fit piece that could lift my spirits.

> *Era già l'ora che volge il disio.*
> *Ai naviganti e intenerisce il cuore.*
> *Lo dì che han detto ai dolci amici addio;*

It was the eighth canto of the Mountain of Purgatory, where the *"peregrin d'amore / Punge, se ode squilla di lontano / Che paia il giorno pianger che si muore."* And as though they wanted to make a fool of me, the church bells, which I suddenly heard from far away, together with the alluring homesickness of the exiled poet, magnified the longing gathered in me into a wave of feeling that made any further work impossible.

To weep for the day that's departing; to lament the day at twilight — except I was not thrown upon the mercy of God. Mariners and pilgrims were under way anyhow, for better or worse; I, on the other hand, was bound as though with chains in a tower.

I had long believed I could busy myself for a few months without having to change places, because nature pushed her motifs like stage sets before my eyes and removed them again, so that every morning I would just have to make a sketch from the same angle of sight to be able, after collecting a week, to transfer the observational and experiential supply of my eye into my oil paintings. But obviously I was not up to the riches of this region, its colors and its degrees of light, or my inner mood was still too weighed down with what, in a Dantesque way, I used to describe as the corpse of my past, which prevented me from giving a pure depiction of what I saw, while at the same time I forgot what I had previously painted. All the tricks that make it possible for someone, even when it doesn't come out right, to paint the rectangle of the canvas in such a way that the critics had something to say and the buyers something to see for their money — it was those very tricks that were so beloved, because you could decipher them, while the real, aloof, and hardly accessible secrets could wait often for years to be discovered. Tricks and ruses — they formed the largest part of contemporary painting, with its fateful inclination to transience, and it was in any event a stable market force only because it was so insanely expensive. Bewildering, but not overwhelming.

Since no one felt sorry for me, I felt sorry for myself, which ran contrary to an optimistic solution of the problem. At first I had been presumptuous and certain of my endeavor, had at once started a large picture in which the size of space and treatment of space were in agreement, but very soon I became involved in details that destroyed the construction of the whole thing.

Suddenly I began to paint fussily realistic tree trunks that had previously intersected the painting as dark courses of color, and after the tree trunks the sky had come to grief, having been designed as chalky and vapid up to then, now taking on a refracted pink, whereby it looked unpleasantly plastic, having no connection with the distance, which in turn contributed a colorful change of the rocks that lay in the foreground and were supposed to form a mute, dark wreath. The picture shrank almost to an uninspired, anecdotal genre painting that would have delighted critics and buyers with its decorative antics, but it left me cold. And gratefully, within myself I had heard "Stop!" brought forth in the tone of a loud command, which finally put an end to the obscene ghost. At the time, not quite four months ago, I found myself in a state of stupid bewilderment that made me afraid of losing my mind over the canvases, followed by a lassitude that had grown stronger in the weeks following, whereupon I worked by doing nothing in order to develop an inner disposition for waiting, the familiarity of stillness. But now things had to happen, now a state should be reached where one is no longer responsible for an event to which one merely lent one's brush for the work in progress.

But even the waiting was kept waiting.

4

Outside, Monsieur Jopin drove past on the tractor with the double tires. He had turned on the windshield wipers, which operated in a curiously quick tempo like a child's toy. What would he think if he saw me at work in the kitchen, but didn't see the car. I didn't have long to wonder, for already he was heading for the tower and waving so that I had to open the window and wave in return. A thick swell of smoke surged in the fresh air past me and was perforated and torn by the rain. For a moment it filled the window so thickly that Monsieur Jopin, with his dark face, looked like a saint on a provincial icon.

"The car's in town," I yelled, as though he had asked me about it. "It wouldn't start."

"Damned weather," was all he said. He leaned his arms on the windowsill and smiled despondently.

Had he noticed that I hadn't been at home the past two days?

"Always by yourself and at work," he said nonchalantly, "that's bad in this weather. If the motif won't show itself you have to seek it out."

He declined an Armagnac, so that suddenly I was left standing with two small thick-bellied glasses, bent over the sink, safe and dry, while the rain dripped from the brim of his hat.

"Well then," he said, and again disappeared on his tractor, which had peacefully rumbled to itself the whole time with a white veil of steam in the air above the motor, which vibrated slightly. I went with both drinks back to the kitchen table. I still couldn't think of work.

"Well then," with that laconic, whispered phrase, Fat Peter had also quit his efforts to convince the woman with the somber distress on her face of his point of view, had thrown a bill furiously onto the bar, without having asked for the check, had whirled his heavy body from the barstool, and gone outside. I still have the clinking in my ear that echoed from the liquor shelf at the closing of the door, a slight, sharp, quickly fading sound.

After his departure the bar had somehow looked impoverished, depopulated and impoverished, for the Dutchmen too had taken off; the jukebox, the glittering main altar, was still, and even the resigned café owner was suddenly no longer present. The woman and I were the only guests. Of course, I, too, should have left, to become at last the radiant innovator of German landscape art; instead, I asked the woman, over the empty barstool, whether I might order her another drink. She was so startled that she stared at me open-mouthed with a fiery-red face.

"Are you German, too?" she asked after a long pause.

And I replied, somewhat too hastily and affectedly: "Something like that."

"Then you did hear that I was left sitting on this barstool," she said defiantly, "and, of course, the reason why as well."

I hadn't heard a thing. Had I been asked what I had been doing for three hours at the bar, I couldn't have

26

answered. Not a thing. I hadn't been doing a thing. During my life I have constantly been asked what I've done or been doing, and never has a satisfactory answer come from me. Distracted waiting, control of a vacuum. My former wife could turn white with anger at my visible oblivion.

"I've been smoking and drinking," I answered finally, slowly, staring directly at her as mockingly as possible. "Besides, I prefer to avoid the arguments of married couples I don't know."

"I don't believe you," the woman said with provocative tenderness. "Everyone listens when his own language is spoken abroad, especially when he can be witness to an argument."

The way she picked up her glass and moved it between her fingers was in bewildering contrast to her somewhat shabby exterior. The thought went through my head: probably she's an actress, maybe too intelligent to be really convincing on the stage, but at any rate not stupid. Anyway, she had a nose one could never forget, a vengeful beak suited to popular melodramas, in which the old story of contempt and longing dissolve into tears that have to be genuine even at the hundredth performance, not pretended.

When I looked up, I saw on her face the certainty that she considered me completely incapable of playing the particular role that she had just thought up for me, which probably had something to do with rescuing her from her awkward predicament.

So I had to say something if I was not to be a flop right from the start, since the play that we intended to perform in this shabby café demanded the right catchword to gain in tempo. I had to step out of my ironic heaviness so that she could become more energetic, more furious. Otherwise the already long-awaited tirade against men would become lame, too tender and thus too unbelievable. I had to insult her in her bleak abandonment, because that was the best method of relieving her of her misfortune — having her become occupied with me. Misfortune for both, for the actress in this provincial comedy and for the painter, who wanted anything but a hopeless love story.

"One of you must pay the price, that's the only thing I overheard. I give you my word."

She laughed. Still, I wasn't sure whether she believed me.

"And what are you doing here among all these ducks in the gloomiest of the French provinces?" she asked me, as the sullen café owner finally had again filled our glasses to complete our intoxication.

"I'm writing a book about Dante."

It was that simple. The lie came out smoothly and point-blank and left no pangs of conscience. In a twinkling I had become a Dante expert. A member of the German Dante Society, who would give the keynote speech at the next Dante Congress and who had stopped off here merely for a ridiculous pastis, by chance, to recover from Paradise.

"You ought to go to Florence," was the only comment on her part, which almost lifted me off my barstool. "However, I did take you at first glance for a painter. For a landscape painter who paints fields and dying beech trees for a German living room."

I tried a cold expression on my face, but felt rather that

I looked apprehensive. Inside, I was too apprehensive to account for my lie and to set it up as a stupid whim; on the other hand, the deception would go up in smoke if she were to visit me in my tower. Apparently I had counted on that.

"Always alone and hard at work," Monsieur Jopin had said. "That's not good in this crummy weather."

So I cried out, "I love painting, I sketch passionately, but as an occupation? There are too many painters, too many pictures, too many galleries and museums, and too many people who consider it their duty to find all that stuff beautiful. I know a painter who wants to haul beauty in with his ruler, and another who has been painting only roof tiles his whole life — moss-covered, crumbled roof tiles in oil and chalk. But that's all futile. What's being painted today is a public nuisance, not a single reinforcing idea lies behind it, only paint, which any fool can spread."

And while I began to let go at length on my favorite theme, she interrupted me again with one of those statements that whizzed down dryly like the blade of a guillotine.

"You not only look like a painter, you talk like one, too."

Her glance, which during my lecture was directed at who knows what sky, now pecked around like a bird at my lie. Naturally I was worried about my inner peace and tried to turn the threatening danger away toward a more profound involvement, but the woman did not allow it and pulled me, resisting, deeper and deeper into her net. Of course, I was inclined to let myself be distracted when my work did not progress, but that an unknown woman was able to disconcert me so quickly had to be linked to the melancholy yearnings that my long-denied isolation had brought into being.

It was dusk when I asked for my check. The café owner had switched on the bar sign, Floc de Gascogne, a gleaming horse with fluttering mane, trying to flee the glow of the light with a mighty leap. Instead of naming a sum, the weary man laid two francs in front of the woman without a word, Fat Peter's change, and I felt like an unexpected guest. She let the money lie there after she had touched the coins lightly with a crooked smile.

5

It seemed ridiculous to me to keep on waiting for the call. Nothing is more humiliating than to stare at a little brown apparatus: *renseignements, réclamations, télégraphe, police-secours-17*. Should I maybe have a talk with the police? I finally poured myself an Armagnac, which I drank with the tiniest sips to drive off the insistent cold that climbed up my legs from the red tiles of the floor. Outside, the sun finally came out and gave back to the landscape the solid contours that had disappeared behind the veil of rain. The water stood in desolate puddles on the path. The ocher-colored fields in front of the house glimmered and steamed. The brain of the earth bathed in the light.

I took a sketching block and chalk, put on a cape, and, hoping against hope, set off on the path down to the river, which I crossed on a small, slippery wooden bridge. Below me the muddy river, in whose currents leaves and trash circled, shot out gurgling. Very soon I reached the clearing that I had selected as a motif, a bright quadrangle in a small wood, sown with molehills, where I had encountered the first live badger of my life. I became aware of a torpor, a stubborn indolence, as though something had taken root in me.

How was I to sketch now, with my hands as heavy as lead? Blue is the color of suffering, I said to myself, but I couldn't do anything with blue. White is the color that keeps the eye healthy. People have nothing blue about them but their eyes. Gray is the color of my eyes. Her eyes are blue, with brown dots in the middle. Water is white, harmony, purity, innocence, the source of everything. White is the repetition of the whole. Completely healthy we will be dead, I cried out in the small clearing, which was spread before me with the most beautiful effects of light and shadow, half-light and reflection, as though it had no need of the crutches of my chalk to make an unforgettable impression.

Was it possible that I had deceived myself so completely?

The life of my eyes seemed to have no more contact with the life of the rest of my body. Eye and hand had broken off their relationship. Ear, nose, everything was independent and obeyed only an emphatic command. What do you hear, I asked my ear, and my nose, what do you smell? Scarcely an answer. Motionless, I squatted there, hardly daring to breathe because I was afraid of falling completely apart. And no one there who could put the precious single parts together again, no hand, no idea, no breath, no name on the forehead, no word. Even the lie of memory that functioned only when moved by shame and humiliation wouldn't get me out of my squat onto my feet. What now, you German landscape painter?

The rain-soaked grass stood in compact clumps and was as thick as fur, now and then hackle and weeds; along the edge, toward the trees, which were framed by hazel bushes, wildflowers bloomed, asserting themselves bravely against the overwhelming green. The birds made an indescribable noise.

For a long time, without moving, I watched the flight of a raptor, which effortlessly, steadily, and regularly crossed over its territory. It had time, took its time; the bickering cries that reached it from below seemed not to touch it. All the less now, when suddenly with a chattering stridency a bird that looked like a shrike plunged into the clearing and pursued a sparrow. In terror the sparrow sprawled flat on the meadow, but was seized, and was mauled by the shrike's beak in such a way that its piteous peeping soon fell silent. Now the victor began to work on it with a fury that I had never seen before. It ripped and plucked at the lifeless sparrow, hacked at it with its beak, hopped squawking about the victim, threw it twitching into the air, and eyed it with a cocked head when it again lay there, frayed to bits and sullied. I came to myself as though recovering from a profound stupefaction, and only after I clapped my hands loudly did it take off with its booty in its talons, but halfway up lost it and probably did not have the courage to turn back again.

Now I ran out into the damp meadow and picked up the bloody remains of the poor sparrow. Under the demented screeching of its own kind — who gave me no peace even when I had finally finished — I sketched it in all its piteousness, with quick strokes, as though the danger existed that this bundle of feathers could be taken away from me. With sober tenacity I had captured the terribly mauled thing with decisive gradations of the chalk: the sheet looked like a picture from another time. The sun had almost sucked up the dampness; from the grass rose a bluish vapor. After an eternity I pulled myself together and vanished like a thief. The big raptor was still circling undisturbed over the clearing.

Sometimes I had the feeling that I needed a disruption, a completely irrevocable disruption to be able to continue the burden of my work and to transform it. No personal excuse could console me for the fact that up to this time I had created a vast pile of scrap paper with my painting, a gilded mediocrity such as is produced everywhere today, a system of allusions and canniness that never really took hold and grasped profoundly. So everybody talked about beauty when they looked at my pictures, about the abstract beauty of the colored surfaces, the lovely proportions. Beauty no longer seizes or confuses the lazy brain, porous feeling, pitiable ignorance. Beauty must come from the other side of death, must have torn something away from death, and the picture must bear witness to that still trembling triumph if it wishes to be a picture and not some bank check or other, a ridiculous impudence in the face of reality. Only when I succeeded in giving shape to the message, the content, the statement that makes everybody laugh, ever more solitary, more isolated, until it hides completely and must be brought into view again with the eyes, in a holy effort, only then would the long wait have made sense. With the picture of the dead sparrow, a new, groping beginning had occurred that somehow led out of my crippled state into life. The substances, the body, the blood-smeared wad of feathers collapsed — the picture triumphed. No woman in the world, and above all not the stranger with the frightful nose, who through her pretended agreement with my desperation had humiliated me more than any other, could prevent me from now bringing to an end what I had begun.

6

When we were standing, slightly inebriated, on the market square, I asked the woman to dine with me. Outside the little town was a small hotel with a restaurant that was marked in the restaurant guide with two forks, a place where I had always wanted to eat. My question as to whether she wanted to go first to her hotel had been answered with a laughing "No. If you like me the way I am, we can go."

I really did like her. Her bony face, her big nose, her deep-seated eyes, her curiously scornful mouth, her awkward gait, her terrible, defensive laugh, the old-fashioned way she was dressed. I liked her very much indeed, and against my will I several times came close to saying so.

"This is the land of the duck," I explained to her solemnly as we were sitting at a corner table in the restaurant. "First, duck pâté, then duck on lettuce, finally breast of duck. A catastrophe for me, because I am determined not to gain weight. Your fat companion would have felt fine here," I added softly, but naturally she had heard it, as she heard everything.

"My business partner," was the curt reply, "my former business partner. His name is Peter, by the way."

"Fat Peter," I said jealously and furiously. We ate the most extravagant and most expensive dish. Afterward came the ridiculous ritual with the Armagnac list. If one left the choice to the waiter, one promptly received the oldest vintage; if one, as a foreigner, made the choice oneself, one received sympathetic glances. Finally a youth with the face of a rabbit wheeled up the bottle cart holding about a hundred bottles.

"What would you like?"

Again it was the strange woman who quickly made a choice and ordered two glasses. It was, of course, the best Armagnac that I had ever drunk in my life.

After the second glass I felt a deep intoxication. The pastis in the town, the aperitif, *pousse rapierre*, a plum liquor with sparkling wine, the red wine, the Armagnac — everything together made me somber and melancholy. I didn't want to talk anymore. I was in such a strangely glum and pensive mood that I decided correctly not to say another word. Nothing about my life, nothing about Dante, nothing about painting. Relieved, I stretched my legs out under the table and with a smile stared at the woman, who now, with the light at her back, looked younger and more venturesome.

"Now you don't want to say anything," she said. "You look like you just decided to keep your mouth shut for a while."

Had she said something? I wasn't sure whether she had just spoken.

Had I asked her name that first evening? My head was humming, but no answer came forth.

In any case, it had been she who suddenly asked the waiter with the big feet whether a room was available. An eternity had passed when the man came back and said, "Yes, for two nights." And when the woman nodded, he had wordlessly laid the key down before her.

Everything had suddenly been so unbelievably easy. After the departure of Fat Peter she had taken charge. Yes, taken charge. She had pulled me from my chair, had laid my arm around her shoulders, and taken me silently past the embarrassed diners to a room on the second floor, up a kind of spiral staircase, pressed me down onto the bed, undressed me, and covered me up.

Miraculous went through my head. A miracle had happened. You don't have to do anything else yourself, don't have to become an innovator in landscape painting or a Dante expert, you just have to submit yourself to the words of this bony woman, then nothing else in the world can happen to you.

And apparently she had also been responsible for the fact that I, the eternal insomniac, had immediately fallen into a deep sleep. But what had the woman told me about herself?

I tried to transfer the drawing of the dead sparrow to a watercolor. The paint box was in the kitchen, so that I could spare myself a depressing trip to the studio. I had to force myself not to think, because the slightest thought threatened to influence the brush that was inclined to surrender to the intensity of an inspired moment. I painted a fallen tree with its roots torn out, the trunk slate blue, with some animated whitish highlights where the light broke up the shadows and created intermediate tones that gave the sheet a dreamy mood. But the dark pits of shadow predominated and gave the slashed bird, with its blood-spattered fluff of feathers, a suggestive space that it didn't get from the harsh, dry system of strokes on the drawing. The watercolor had a more succinct effect, more final; the ghostly impression of emptiness and fear increased with color. A picture of death, from which such an intense sadness emanated that, overcome by my own work, I had to lay it aside quickly.

I tried Dante again, so that the day wouldn't pass completely without literary work, but after the sparrow watercolor not much could be created. My memory of the past two days was cranked up again and toiled feverishly, without arriving at any kind of result.

Ma non eran da ciò le proprie penne —

but my own wings weren't up to that; however, my mood was suddenly convulsed by a glistening light, whereupon its wish was fulfilled. Exalted fantasy was abandoned by vigor; now my longing and my desiring resembled a wheel that turns steadily, driven by love, which moves the sun and all the other stars.

But I could not think of the rhymes, no matter how carefully I played with the words. Give it up, I told myself, nothing else is possible today. I took the book up to the second floor, lay down on the bed, and pulled the fur blanket up to my ears. Nobody is as alone on this earth as I, I thought self-pityingly, but was not able to enjoy the tugging feeling very long because I sensed sleep pulling me into a long dark tunnel. I let it happen.

7

The history of the literature on Dante continually produces scholars who impudently champion the assertion that Beatrice never existed.

"Between Beatrice and you is only this wall," says Virgil. This wall of sleep behind which her goodness flares, and her inexhaustible humility. Rest at this wall, lie down in the dust with the thistles and wait. To your left spreads a green sea on which a brown boat softly bobs on the waves, a wooden eye. To your right four olive trees, planted at an equal distance, rise up from the sandy soil; they give you shade when the sun is high. Before you, nothing but the wall, built with flat Roman brick, behind it the open, luminous, and exalted place.

There is no landscape in the usual sense that could be painted. I have stared my eyes blind, until they became irritated and were shot with red, but nothing I have seen produced a picture. I have seen algae on the rocks, their reddish shimmer, the shimmering dampness over the clumps of earth, the light that surrounds the oaks, but that did not produce a landscape. A wall always stood between me and the landscape, a high brick wall, and I knew that behind it something began that I would never be able to paint.

8

It was a little before eight when I woke up with a hangover. The fields in the plain lay weary and severe. A breath of milky brightness still lay over the hills, as though to prove to me that it was still daylight, the day on which the woman had abandoned me so unceremoniously. Anyway, it was no longer raining. If I were to put on my rubber boots, I could still take a long evening walk, and perhaps I would see an owl. Owls bring good luck. I stuck out my foot and with my big toe turned on the television set, whose light filled the room immediately. The news.

An insistent woman was sitting in the room already, in a close-up, telling about the difficulties that French children are having with the reformed spelling. So nothing bad has happened, I thought; it's only that the children cannot decide whether a certain word is written with *t* or still with *th*. But then the first dead came into the picture, in Lebanon, in the zones occupied by Israel, in Guatemala, where a hotel had collapsed in front of the camera's eye. Somewhere a drug war had broken out again, but I had not understood the name of the country; gently heaped mountains of cocaine were shown and surly soldiers looked on, guarding it with fixed bayonets. A young, toothless woman explained tearfully that the cultivation of cocaine was her only support. Heartrendingly she pointed at two dirty children, who were staring at her with big eyes.

And then suddenly the German chancellor, who had dismissed his party secretary, was in my room. "No speculations, please, about political differences, please," I heard him say, before the nasal French voice of the commentator chimed in again, "He is only fifty-nine years old — no respect for age, like everywhere." In his youth even the chancellor must have had his head stroked by his father and heard him say that he should think about the fact that one day he would have to take the responsibility for the whole German fatherland. He had always thought of that when the other boys wanted to play cards. And now he is the federal chancellor and can dismiss the party secretary unconditionally. What might my unknown lady friend have said, if the federal chancellor had invited her to Pierre's for a pastis? You don't look like the federal chancellor, more like a German landscape painter? Thank God the man became chancellor, otherwise he probably would have had to drink his pastis alone, I thought.

The party secretary, who then appeared and looked significantly younger than the chancellor, opposed his dismissal. "A step in the wrong direction," he said, and the commentator translated the expression correctly into French. There's no end to the absurdity when the somber men stand next to one another. How funny and awkwardly grim both the gentlemen are, I thought, like bad actors, compared to the rhetoric of the French prime minister, who is immediately queried about the problem of the foreign workers. Before the weather forecast came on, the police requested the help of the viewers. On French television, which was best watched with the sound turned off, in order to follow all the nuances, this was when one had the best chance of forming an impression.

A policeman explained that another policeman had been murdered, in Toulouse. Killing a policeman is prohibited in France, of course, but when a foreigner murders a policeman, he must count on additional vexations. And in this case they were of the opinion that a foreigner was involved. An Arab, no doubt, I thought, when suddenly the "wanted" picture appeared.

A thick face filled the television screen almost completely, a bullish face with swollen eyes. "Fat Peter," went through my head, "that's Fat Peter," and in my stupid drowsiness I moved very close to the screen in order to look into his police-sketch eyes. But the picture had already vanished, and an unbelievably vain type with a massive mustache explained about the clouds we should expect as a passing phenomenon.

I turned the sound down and stared into space. Had some unnoticed turn in my life pulled me into a plot? Had I wasted the possibility of finishing my pictures because of the ridiculous chance of having invited a strange, recently-abandoned woman for a pastis? "It wasn't Fat Peter," I said out loud, "such a fat man is in no shape to murder a French policeman and then to flee. He can abandon women, torture June bugs, cheat on his taxes, but he just can't shoot down a human being with a pistol." And with these words of reassurance I went decisively upstairs into my studio and at once began to work.

It went better than expected. Despite a keen hunger, I worked steadfastly, as though the slightest diversion would mean the disruption of the whole project. In great sweeps and with ribbons of paint I filled up several canvases that I planned to work on in the following days. But the idea of the project suddenly took shape, and it corresponded exactly to the idea that I had had before beginning my journey. My hand worked automatically. Apparently I had needed all the peace and preparation to finally paint so easily.

The critics had classified my last exhibition as too intellectual, as though to be a painter and a conceptualist simultaneously were forbidden, and although as a rule I paid no attention to critics, that judgment, which was meant as reproach, got to me. My colleagues, whom I saw occasionally, were pure painters. They never read a book, had hardly any interest in the history of art, and whenever it came to an aesthetic exchange, they always referred to the creation, the deed. Some of them — and not the worst in my opinion — professed an aestheticism of the act and laughed at my worries. Concepts are thieves, they rob you of the truth of your picture. "Don't think about it, do it," they had advised me when I wanted to discuss the criticism of my last exhibition. So now I painted, painted as though possessed, let the brush glide unimpeded over the canvas as though there were no resistance to truth.

It was already well past midnight when the telephone rang. It was downstairs in the kitchen. At first I didn't want to answer it, then I persuaded myself that it would stop ringing by the time I got downstairs, but it didn't stop. Communication is the end of creativity. So I started running, jumped down the last steps, and tore the instrument from its cradle. The woman, I thought, finally it's the woman!

It was my gallery owner. "Why so out of breath?" he asked. "I just wanted to hear how you are doing."

He was sitting with a few clients after one of his terrible openings and talk had come around to me. A collector, a sausage manufacturer in Saarbrücken, had asked about me; now they were calling me in their beery mood to find out whether I was really at work. "I'll give you Herr Scheibe," said my gallery owner over my protests, "tell him yourself what you're doing."

And then the sausage manufacturer was really on the line, a nice fellow who had once told me why he bought all the pictures that were hanging in his house. It was a long, banal story that ended with a frightful intoxication. But since then he had bought one of my pictures every year for his villa in Saarbrücken, which was stuffed to the attic with canvases in all styles.

"I'm driving to Toulouse next month," I heard him yell. "Should I look in at the tower?"

"Sure," I said, not to vex him, "there's a small hotel with a restaurant nearby where I can put you up." I gave him the exact address and telephone number and then said that he ought to bring along his rubber boots so we could go on a hike.

"And I'll bring along a rifle, too, so we can defend ourselves against any angry French policemen," he said laughing, as though he had told a great joke.

A rifle?

Actually, over German television, there had been a

report not only about the dismissal of the party secretary, but also about the murder of a policeman in the vicinity of Toulouse in which a German was said to have been involved.

"But he was much fatter than you," the sausage manufacturer yelled in my ear, "unless you've gained weight from eating the Gascogne ducks."

"Oh, well," I said brusquely and ended the conversation without waiting for my gallery owner, who wanted to speak to me again.

Fat Peter. The fat pig in his custom-made suit had shot down a policeman. And I was caught in a trap because the unknown woman had driven off in my car the previous morning without leaving an address. You should never consort with people who are out for adventure. Adventurers will be the death of me. Through no acts of my own a fairly large turning point in my life had taken place and there had to be a way I could get out of it.

9

The night was horrible. First of all, I couldn't get to sleep because I kept remembering the second day with the unknown woman, every detail. Then, dreams tortured me. Finally, a late-night mosquito.

Nothing had happened on the two happiest days of my life. I had woken up in the strange hotel room, had looked around confused and had a coughing fit, and suddenly through the veil in front of my eyes caught sight of the woman, who was sitting peacefully in the armchair in front of the window, reading a book in the morning sun, which fell in two equal surfaces on the floor. It doesn't happen often in life that you wake up and think, you're saved. But it was just like that. At the sight of the woman reading in the morning sun, I felt saved. It looked like a picture by Vermeer, strictly articulated and still mysterious. With the Hollander the source of the light remains uncertain, and that's the way it had been in the hotel room.

"What are you reading?" was my first question, if I remember correctly. Not an especially intelligent question to an unknown woman in the morning.

"A Belgian novel," she said, and held up the book. "It was in the bedside table."

"In what language?"

"It looks like Spanish to me."

"Do you speak Spanish?"

"In my profession you have to speak all languages," she said, "even the common ones."

I had asked no further questions because my knowledge of languages is quite spotty; besides, there were too many riddles in her reply. She had said, "In my profession. . ."

She had already been to town that morning, had bought a toothbrush and shampoo, *Le Monde* and the *Bild*, the latter two days old and the only German newspaper that could occasionally be found here. What impression would one have of Germany if there were only this newspaper? One shouldn't form impressions.

The former news commentator of German television, Herr Köpcke, had been more or less torn to pieces by his own dog, a peaceful animal up to that time. Without the daily reports of his master, the dog had gone mad; without the rhythm of repetition, insanity increases. Of course, I knew Herr Köpcke well. He had a cultivated way of speaking, not to the extent of my mustachioed, favorite commentator Gerhard Klarner, but near enough. I reviewed Herr Köpcke's movements as he laid the sheet of paper aside during bad news that was followed by a picture report, shaking his inclined head delicately. "The talks are still going on at this hour." Picking up the sheet at "talks," laying it down at "on," looking at the viewer, not at the sheet, and shaking his head gently until the picture appeared. That was the manner of Herr Köpcke, who had now been torn almost completely apart by his Doberman.

"Poor devil," I said, "he was better known than the ex-chancellor. The one is torn apart by dogs in his row house

48

while the other sits with his wife Loki on the shore of Lake Brahm and is said even to take money for interviews."

The strange woman laughed, as I went muttering into the bathroom. And when, scrubbed, I stepped back into the room, breakfast was already on the table. The woman could perform magic, transform things; I was continually the astonished onlooker.

But the suggestion to drive to Moissac came from me. I wanted to show her the tympanum, not least of all to have the opportunity to explain something to her. She drove. She wanted very much to try out the Citroën, called the Duck, a rattletrap that my friend had lent me. She drove worse than either of my wives, but was self-assured, and I sat quietly satisfied beside her without giving advice, despite my inborn inability to enjoy the commonalty of life. It sounded horrible, the way she put the car into gear; it trembled and groaned, but finally we arrived in Moissac.

For a whole hour we stood in front of the abbey church St.-Pierre, facing the Majestas Domini that looked stonily down upon us. The elders of the Apocalypse craned their necks with effort; the prophet Jeremiah with his too-long beard looked on unhappily; Lazarus had collapsed; the Devil with his body thrust forward beset Luxuria, from whose breasts snakes crawled. I explained the friezes over the arcade and every individual capital, from Samson and the lion to Daniel in the lions' den.

She fell in love at once with the Abbot Durandus because he had such beautiful hands. Two fingers of his right hand were stretched out, two were bent, the thumb stood aside, as is proper. In his left hand he held the shepherd's staff. Although it was a relief, the abbot gave a pretty robust impression — his face, especially, gave no hint of asceticism. He looks like Fat Peter, I was about to say, but controlled myself. When I reached the ornamental and figurative conceptions and compositional schemes, she interrupted me.

"If you talk like that about Dante," she said, "no one will want to speak after you at your congress."

Everything had been so simple. And while I tossed sleeplessly in my bed and battled the mosquito, which was able to escape every slap, I saw the woman before me so precisely that I wanted to touch her bony face with my hands. I wanted to protect her, wanted to warn her, but she only smiled her sad, ironic smile and vanished.

I turned on the lamp; it was a little before four in the morning; it was ice-cold in the room. Dante had to be of aid, the inexhaustible fount. I opened a translation done in the twentieth century at random and read a few verses of the fourth canto of *Purgatorio*:

> When through delight or it may be through pain
>> Conceived by some one faculty of ours,
>> That faculty doth all the soul enchain,
> It seems it gives heed to no other powers;
>> And this refutes that error which believes
>> That in us one soul over another flowers;
> So when the soul by the ear or the eye receives
>> What grapples it and strongly clings it round,
>> Time goes, and naught of it the man perceives.
> For 'tis one power that listens to the sound

And another that which keeps the soul entire:
This one is still at large, and that one bound.

It can't be better translated, nor expressed more clearly, nor describe my situation more exactly, I thought. Then I must finally have fallen asleep.

10

A banging on the door woke me with a start. In my under-wear I went down the steps drunk with sleep and opened the door. It was Monsieur Jopin, bringing me my mail, which he wanted to hand me himself and not, as usual, put on the kitchen table. Another death notice already. A short time before I had been elected to the Academy, which sent its members a death notice about twice a month and a budgetary item that was discussed at great length at each meeting.

At home I hung the black-bordered notices on a molding in my studio, where they formed a small, fluttering shrine. Nothing but intellectual giants from philosophy and literature, a few actors, and some graphic artists. One day I will be hanging there, too, I often thought. That's the fate of all the members of the Academy. You are slowly prepared for that, notice by notice. You ought to hurry up with your work — so I understood the message of the black-bordered notices — or else it will be too late for your magnum opus.

An acquaintance of mine, a philosopher, had resigned from the Academy because he was afraid of one day receiv-ing his own death notice. My election had been noted nega-tively in the press by a critic who would himself have liked to become a member of the Academy and a recipient of its death notices. He foamed at the mouth. My wife at the time was already afraid that the prices for my paintings would fall, the man had made such mincemeat of me. But the opposite happened, I had never received so many offers for exhibitions as then. At one of those openings I met him again, amiable, obliging, and very witty.

"You have me to thank for this success," he said highhandedly. "Without my attack nobody would have given you a second glance."

"That's right," I had answered, because nothing else occurred to me.

"Exactly," he said. He had immediately had his polemic against me printed in a book, as he informed me, beaming with joy, so that my run of good luck would continue. "I am your shadow," he had said. "As long as I pursue you, you will be successful, that's the way it is with all the artists whom I smash critically." It was a long evening, because you can't get rid of your shadow.

At parting we embraced, and he promised to write another biting critique, which he then actually did. And the gallery actually sold all the paintings, and the drawings as well. Since then he has written only speeches in gratitude for all the critics' prizes that have been bestowed upon him, and now he is a member of every imaginable academy, but not the one that had Monsieur Jopin bring me the sad news of the death of another member.

"A relative?" asked Monsieur Jopin with a hangdog expression.

"Yes," I lied, "a close relative. I'll probably have to drive to the funeral in Germany."

At this murmured statement Monsieur Jopin was all

ears. He seemed completely changed to me on that gray and damp morning, and I found out the reason at once.

"The police were in town," he said, "and asked about your friend. A policeman was shot to death around here, by a foreigner. Now they're checking all the foreigners who live in the area." At these words he pulled the local newspaper from his jacket and held it under my nose. The police sketch of the fat man who was being sought as the supposed murderer appeared on the front page.

"Looks like a Belgian," I said indifferently.

"Yes, either a Belgian or a German," said Monsieur Jopin, even though the face could also have fitted a Frenchman. Assignment to a locality was ticklish with fat faces. A fat Swede can hardly be distinguished from a fat Swiss. Characteristics begin only under the lard.

"Were the police at your place?"

To the question of the police about where my friend could be reached he had answered, in South America, but I, the man in the tower, would certainly know more exactly.

"They'll be coming along for sure," he said, morose all of a sudden, and turned abruptly to the door, where, however, he stopped again. "By the way, I'll be driving to town later. Perhaps if you want to come along, to pick up the car."

"The car," I said, confused. "Yes, I'll be at the house about eleven."

"About ten-thirty," said Monsieur Jopin, already half a policeman, and left.

The car.

We had returned in the late afternoon, had filled our gas

tank along the way, stopped then in Moncrabeau at the Phare, and had devoured another all-duck dinner along with a Buzet, and afterward Armagnac again, and had arrived at the hotel about eleven, dog-tired. During the entire trip back I had looked at the strange woman from the side. Looked at her, not examined her. There are faces that never mature. But this face, which looked into the evening so cheerfully, seemed incapable of change. I imagined it without skin, without lips and eyes. Without hair. But it always remained the same face, as long as I couldn't imagine it without a nose.

"Great humanists had a partiality for noses, small ones kept to ears. You've heard that already?"

"No, but I smell a rat. You're probably studying my nose," she had said. "It turned out a little too long. Bad for police posters, if you're the one wanted."

"I hope no one finds you," I had answered.

"Why?"

"So I won't lose you. It's comforting to have a chauffeur; nobody wants to work as a chauffeur anymore."

"I noticed exactly how you suffer when I change gears," she had said.

"Yes," I admitted, "we'll have to buy a new car, with an automatic transmission."

"And then you can sit in the backseat under the reading light and study Dante while I chauffeur you to Florence."

We'd had another at the bar, then had gone up to the room and showered, because, as she said, "We probably smell like our clothes," and then had gone to bed. To our beds, to be exact, for two beds stood in the room, separated by a small chest.

"Well intentioned," she had said, when I spoke to her about that ugly piece of furniture, "but any object can be overcome."

And in the morning, when I woke up, she was gone.

"She'll have gone into town to get a newspaper," I had said to myself in the bathroom mirror, to give me courage against my increasing anxiety. No mirror, no face.

"She'll be right back with breakfast," I had whispered to myself when I was sitting on her chair in front of the window, staring into the light rain. I had even picked up the novel, a story about a Dutch doctor who one day out of the clear blue sky had shot his wife and her inconsiderate lover to death, as I translated from the back of the book. In his peaceful life in the country there had also come a sudden turning point, I thought to myself, but perhaps he also had good reasons to take up his weapon. You have to shoot women when they jump their traces; Dutch women, I had immediately corrected myself.

Afterward I had sat silently, so as to be inconspicuous, and had hardly breathed. If you become really little and are on the point of disappearing forever into a crack in the floor, she'll come through the door and rescue you. She'll grab you by the hair and pull you up carefully. I had to get hold of myself so as not to get silly. Everyone wants things to be fine, so it has to be awful for me. Near twelve the front desk called and asked whether I wanted to extend my stay another night.

No, I didn't want to.

I stared at the wall, on which a bizarre damp spot had formed, a gray, circular mollusk that turned yellow at its edges. They ought to put a frame on it and, instead of removing it, get rid of the awful picture hanging over the bed, an old advertisement for regional products. Early Nay, late Michaux, or the other way around.

The porter gave me a slip of paper on which she excused herself for taking the car. Unfortunately she had to get going. There was nothing else to do. Until later.

A handwriting with jutting descenders, as though the writer were sweeping something from the table, making it disappear, with small hooks at the end, as though she doubted her resolution.

I paid and walked back in the rain across the fields to my tower. That's all, Forrestal, and that's that, kitty-cat.

"And what was the lady's name?" I could hear my mother ask.

And my father saying, "She wasn't so dumb if she left you sitting there with egg on your face."

Me, their son, the painter.

It was half-past nine, I had another hour of work. Not enough time to go into the studio, so I opened the door and studied the landscape.

There were mornings now that were already like late-autumn days. An aroma of smoke and wet earth lay in the air. The purity, the liberation of the first weeks of September — in which, in contrast to painting, thought was easy because everything superfluous, unessential, disappeared in the clarity of the atmosphere — had been transformed into hazy monotony. After a few yards the path led toward an invisible dissolution, and the boulders looked unreal, eerie, and unstable, as though they were about to roll off at any moment. Nothing was more natural.

Even I do not believe in stones in any sort of strong, religious sense, in damp wood and steaming earth, but still those were the things that were anchored fast in my worldview about painting. Again and again I had drawn their portrait — the lichen, white and dried, with a darker, still-damp center; the bright green dots of last year's moss; the wet, little gray black balls of earth and fiber in which whole populations of beetles lived, tiny little animals that moved off as though on rollers, when you got too close with your finger; and finally the spreading yellow growth on the stones that exuded a pigment more glowing than anything I had ever seen.

One part of these surroundings belonged to my world, another part to another world. Except that the boundaries became indistinct when you had an almost fraternal association with these things for too long. For example, where did the rusty plow belong, whose dark blades had served me heretofore as an anecdotal utensil but now had the effect of a sign that I should receive: like an object withdrawn from time, looming up from a tellurian distance.

For many years I had grappled with aesthetic problems but never wasted many thoughts on myself in particular because that kind of narcissism had always offended me. First the picture, then me. If the picture was successful, then, exhausted, I came into view. On the other hand, I can now say in good conscience that I don't know who I am. When I produced something, only one soul was at work within me, to speak with Dante's words. All other powers were simply subsouls, auxiliary gods, have-nots that had only attending functions. As a matter of fact, no one has ever asked me who I am, because such questions are not those that taciturn people employ. And my sorrows had never reached so great a magnitude that I was forced to seek their causes and burden other people with them. I had gone astray, not in a sickly way, but in a healthy, absolutely natural way that would have repulsed any psychologist, and I felt no deficiency because of that. And as long as I painted, this condition was the most pleasant because painting could hold sway over me effortlessly without encountering any resistance worth mentioning. Despite two marriages, my ego, if there is such a thing deserving of the name, was the quiet, almost immaterialized center of a vortex, and I was the only one who could express the vortex, could paint it, without immediately wasting my psychic energy. If this painting was called intellectual, that was all right with me.

Why in the world did something have to change now?

It was uncomfortable to stand suddenly on the edge of existence in such perplexity. Why should I make a choice when I could not influence what happened?

But I had to make a choice; the strange woman had inconsiderately forced me to do so. And as I was thinking about this, I felt the smooth stone of the threshold under my feet, the dependable, never wobbling stone.

11

Monsieur Jopin was already sitting in his car when I came over the hill that separated the tower from the house. He always wore dark blue shirts and black corduroy jackets and smoked yellow Gitanes, which — as in the good old days that he embodied and defended — he only touched twice, once when he stuck them in his mouth and again when he picked the remains of the wheat paper from his lips. With a few words he could explain the mysteries of agriculture and the weather, of owls and ducks, so that, despite the ungainly dialect, one was completely certain that one had understood everything. He did not dare become my enemy because of the vanished car. Above all, there was still Madame Jopin, his mother, who had something against Germans for good reason. She had been a member of the resistance; her husband had been shot to death by Germans in a neighboring village. On Sundays she went to church with a decoration on her jacket that had been bestowed upon her — personally — by de Gaulle.

"Are you married?" Monsieur Jopin had once asked me, and before I could come out with the complicated truth, he had said, "I can't manage it, because of her." So he had stayed a bachelor and lived with the proud old woman in a house on the estate, from which a sharp smell of goats came when one walked past the door, which was always open. On holidays and on weekends his illegitimate daughter, Jacqueline, who lived with her mother in Toulouse, visited him, and on many evenings the overseers of other estates came to discuss technical problems and drink a glass of wine, but as a rule he lived alone with the gloomy old woman.

Silently we drove into town. In front of the Citroën repair shop he let me get out because he wanted to drive on to the co-op, where today they were going to discuss their experiences with soybeans. There were fields where up to this time, because of the condition of the soil, only wheat had been cultivated in an unbroken sequence. Now he wanted to suggest a changing crop sequence to my friend. Did I imagine it or did he really grin, when he said good-bye to me? Perhaps he was thinking that I already had one foot behind bars. Thank God there was no jail in this place where they could throw me so I might reflect on where a Citroën 2 CV could be.

Actually, there was nothing in the place that could interest me. No marketplace, no people. There was the church, of course, which had been put up in the seventeenth century, but I wasn't interested in churches. So, to the newsstand. I bought copies of all the day's newspapers, including the *Sport Press*, which got me a curious glance from the salesclerk. And now the café. Would I succeed in entering the café standing tall and without being nervous, the place where my happiness and the misfortune that followed on its heels had had their beginnings?

Monsieur Pierre was, in fact, astonished to see me in his café so early. I was the only customer; the next ones would come only at midday, after twelve.

"Coffee," I said, and he seemed glad to be allowed to work at his machine, his back turned to me. On the counter lay the *Dispatch*, which he had just been reading.

"Not a trace of the murderer," said the café owner. "A German," and with that he set my coffee down next to the newspaper.

"Or a Dutchman," I said. No comment. He took his paper and withdrew to one of the tables; I sat down with my pile at another. So we sat silently opposite one another and studied the murder case. Drugs were involved, as usual. Money, not ideals. While handing over drugs for cash at a rest stop near Toulouse, the police undercover man had gotten nervous and drawn his pistol, but the other man had been quicker. Only after giving an exact description of the gunman had the policeman died in the hospital. His name wasn't mentioned, for reasons of security, but a picture of his family was printed, a thin woman with two children who were staring anxiously at their mother. "Your father is dead," the mother must have just said, "shot to death by a drug dealer. By a German. Or by a Dutchman, your father wasn't able to identify the accent that precisely."

"What will you do now?" the intelligent reporter from the *Dispatch* had asked the woman.

"Nothing" was her reply: "*rien.*"

The police were searching for the men behind the operation in Marseilles, Rotterdam, and Cologne — a whole ring. Interpol had been brought in. Raids had produced nothing. Monsieur K., as the fat man was called, could not be found, but was presumed to be in the country still.

"He looks just like the guy you were drinking with at the bar," the café owner suddenly started the match.

"Yeah," I said.

"Was he a German?"

"I think so."

"Did he speak German?"

"Yeah, pretty good."

"So he was a German," the café owner concluded the first round, which clearly went to him. Quiet prevailed for a while, until the rustling of the newspaper, the bell for the second round.

"Where is the woman you kept drinking with, anyway?"

"No idea," I said.

"A German?"

"Yeah."

"You ought to go to the police and make a statement," he now recommended. "Maybe they could catch the murderer then."

"Now that's enough!" I said. "In the first place, I didn't know either the man or the woman personally. In the second place they could be harmless tourists."

"But he didn't look like a tourist," came from the café owner's corner, "more like a drug dealer."

I walked to his table and laid six francs next to the paper. "For the coffee."

Without looking up from his paper, he pushed the money aside as though he wanted to have nothing to do with an accomplice to a crime.

"You live in the tower behind Grazimis," he said suddenly, now completely Pierre the Detective, "at that German's place."

"That I do," I said. "Good-bye."

I had myself driven home in the only taxi in the place. The taxi driver, too, delivered a lecture on the murder incident. "To Grazimis?" he asked. "To the German's place? Were the police there already? Maybe he's not growing wheat at all. Does Jopin still work up there?"

I let him chatter on and stared quietly across the fields, whose color was darker after the heavy rain the day before. After the plowing Monsieur Jopin had worked them again with a harrow, so that the heavy clods disappeared and the seed that was to be planted next would get into the earth better. Now the heavy clay soil looked as finely raked as a vegetable bed.

I loved this landscape, and as a sign of my devotion I wanted to dedicate a series of paintings in large format to it, which in German villas would be proof of the fame of the *département* of Gers.

I had the taxi stop halfway home because I wanted to walk the rest of the way along the river, which wound northward next to the train tracks. Here small gardens were laid out everywhere, punctiliously measured and making use of every speck of earth, as though their owners wanted to build a bulwark against the ever-increasing *zone industrielle* that, on the other side of the river, formed an imposing panorama with gigantic, ugly metal sheds. A chimney gave off a mighty column of smoke that broke apart and unraveled a few yards above it; out of another a smoking flame flared up.

A repulsive stench lay over the peaceful valley. Several times I almost slid down on the greasy, slippery plants that covered the path maliciously, but the luck of the distracted always let me regain my balance. I wanted to remember details, specific gestures, her laughter that drew small creases about her big nose, but I could capture nothing. She was present and absent in a weird way, and if circumstances had not indicated that she had duped me with her physical presence, I would have taken her for a real ghost.

Suddenly in front of me rose the industrial cathedral, a light brown monster whose monumental weight smothered the region. A silo or storehouse of corrugated sheet metal. To lessen the frightful sight, they had supplied it with a thick corset of bushes, which, however, were decorated with paper and other trash. If I wanted to get home, I had to walk over a wooden bridge, cross the road, and climb the hill across an empty wheat field. But I walked on, because at the next turn of the river lived an English couple whom I occasionally visited and now absolutely had to see. Apparently the time of my healthy solitude was past.

12

Paul was a writer. Marina managed the household, took care of the garden, and was a goose-liver pastry specialist. Their daughter, Emily, a friend of Monsieur Jopin's daughter, studied medicine in Toulouse. Their house was covered with grapevines that they had trained to run horizontally on trellises, so that the property looked like one in provincial England. It exuded something unpretentiously charming, a quality otherwise absent in the area.

Marina already knew all about my predicament. Her gentle confidence was hard to bear because it lacked any ingredient of fantasy. Everything was checked off, as on a shopping list: car gone, woman gone, fat German gone, peace of mind gone, work gone to hell.

"That's the way it is," I said, and was glad when Paul appeared in the doorway, his cold pipe in his mouth and a book in his hand. *A Schoolmaster with the Blackfoot Indians*, a wonderful book, he'd say at once, because he found everything wonderful, even my paintings — though not his own books, from the American sale of which they could live well. Recently he had been reading Dante at my instigation, although his English Dante didn't sound at all like my German Dante, and I had trouble translating his quotations. "I see clearly," he said, "that your mind will never have enough, unless truth illuminates it, beyond which there is no truth."

"*Paradiso*, third canto," I said finally, and he nodded amiably, although we both knew that something more was implied.

"Everything will be cleared up," said Paul, "if you're innocent. In the opposite case, you ought to erase your traces. We aren't put in this world to be asked questions, particularly not by the French police."

Paul hated new experiences. "New experiences just distract you," was his pronouncement. "Anyone who collects experiences cannot write a decent book. Besides, after every very intense experience you'd have to be different," he asserted, "and take a different name. That's bad for a writer."

When Marina traveled to England to sell one of his new manuscripts, she left stamped envelopes at the newsstand so that Paul received his television guide on time. He never went into the city anymore because he dreaded a new experience, but he liked to be told what new fad people had taken up. "Good that I don't have to see that," was his comment. His character, too, was managed by Marina — he himself, in his opinion, didn't know how to handle it. When you no longer expose yourself to new experiences, it is comforting if someone who knows you well looks after your character. He often said, "People who want to know who they are are weird to us. Too much character spoils a manuscript, then the advances decline." Thank God he was one of those who never give anyone their own books to read; it sufficed to inspect the cover when a package with paperback editions arrived. "Wonderful," said Paul, took the books, and carried them into the shed, where mountains of old author's copies were moldering next to the goat pen. The remarkable animal with its overlarge udders gaped yellow-eyed at the disintegrating pile of books and bleated in fright when it became larger again. "My most merciless critic," commented the Englishman, who liked to hold an author's copy under its pink nose and could laugh to beat all at the expression of revulsion and repugnance that formed instantly on the goat's face.

"You shouldn't have invited the woman to dinner," he now said. "Women who argue with men in public aren't worth anything. They're obstinate, they steal, they're greedy. If you had read my books, that wouldn't have happened to you. Reading saves you from bad experiences. A great part of world literature has been written to warn against women; the rest warns against them unintentionally. From *Antigone* to *Madame Bovary*, a library of abominations, deceit, murder, adultery, suffering. It always begins harmlessly with a meal. In the end the car is gone, and peace and quiet is done for."

"What should I do now?"

"Paint the woman's nose," said Marina, "then you'll be cured forever."

It began to rain again when I started home. The rain fell evenly, quietly, unperturbed. It is one of the tactless characteristics of weather to reinforce one's frame of mind, and not only in literature.

13

In front of the tower, visible from afar, a police car. It looked so out of place in this landscape that I would have preferred to paint it over. With brown sienna to make it fit in with the fields. At the door stood two policemen and a man in street clothes, all three acting as though they hadn't been in the house.

"Hello," I said, "the door isn't locked, as you probably know." They laughed. Four together, we entered the kitchen, where on the table lay several copies of *The Divine Comedy*, in addition to a typewriter and a lot of paper. It looks like work, I thought; that'll make an impression.

It turned out that they knew everything. The café owner had talked, the hotel porter, even Monsieur Jopin, the brooding eccentric, had not exactly remained quiet. It was nice not to have to lie, but that didn't improve the story.

"You don't know the name of the woman you spent two nights with in the Hotel Printemps?"

"No."

"Can you describe her?"

Boy, could I! For a whole quarter hour I described the two happiest days of my life in every detail, reconstructed our conversations, our drive to Moissac, the nights.

"And you never asked her what her name was?"

"We had no time for such trivialities."

Actually, I had been tempted several times to ask what

her name was but had always dropped it. As long as she was there, she didn't need a name, but now I would like to have known it myself so I could call her up.

"A name is not a triviality," said one of the policemen bluntly.

"But it is," I said, "completely superfluous. Even *your* name is without importance, arbitrarily established on the day after your birth, when your father was sitting with his pals in a bar. Pierre or Henri, what difference does that make?"

"My name is Jacques," said the policeman, "and I don't want to be addressed as Pierre. And if someone calls me Henri, I don't answer."

"Toulouse isn't called Paris," said the other policeman, "and Paris is not Brest."

"And we're in Grazimis, not in Frankfurt," said the first, proud of his observation. "Everything has a name here."

"And you didn't report to the police the theft of your car, your friend's car?" the man in street clothes asked.

"It wasn't stolen," I said. "She just borrowed it and she'll bring it back, I'm completely convinced of that. A woman like her doesn't steal a 2 CV. Besides, I would gladly give it to her and buy my acquaintance a new one."

"Where is your acquaintance?"

"In South America."

"Have you heard from him?"

"No, he planned to be back in the spring."

"And the man in the police sketch doesn't remind you

of the man with whom you had a conversation in Pierre's café?"

It was tiresome not to have to lie.

"We would like to ask that you not leave the country without informing us," said the man in street clothes. "Did you plan to drive to Germany for a funeral?"

"No," I said, "the funeral has surely already taken place. Mail is too slow for funerals."

"And call us when you believe you must report the car stolen."

"Even if it's returned?" I asked.

"Absolutely," said the detective in street clothes, "even if it's returned."

And with that the questioning was finished.

Through the kitchen window I saw the blue car drive away. Cars do not belong in this landscape, only ducks do.

When they had vanished, I noticed that the farewell letter of the strange woman, which I had fastened with a magnet onto the refrigerator, had likewise vanished, the only thing that bound me physically to her. We are separated, my dear; now everyday life begins again. I went up to my studio immediately and began to work in a frenzy.

14

I worked. Work sounds so ordinary, so regulated according to lunch time and quitting time. I worked as though possessed, as though the world, whose last witness I was, were about to disappear. Until sundown I stood in the studio, painting. My back hurt so that I sometimes had to scream loudly to drive away the pangs for a short time. My right hand was stiff in the morning and had to be bathed in chamomile, massaged in the evenings with arnica. Then came stomachaches. My eyes were irritated and shot with red by the steady increase of smoke. And still the long hours seemed to me the most productive of my life.

On the heels of the two happiest days of my life now followed the most productive four weeks, in which powerful paintings came into being. Naturally I was aware of the circumstance that one thing had something to do with the other, at least in the beginning. In the conversations I had out loud with myself, I made fun of myself, lauded the productive betrayal of love, praised the woman who, thank God, had left me, so that my work was finally becoming reality. Had you remained, stranger without a name, there would have been no paintings, only froth.

But this euphoric condition didn't last long, for what developed next was deeper, coming out of darker layers into daylight. Like a southern brook that, after a long, dry summer, suddenly breaks forth from a pebbly slope and within a few weeks swells to a rushing stream, that's how it flowed from me. I had been empty, completely empty, burned out and eviscerated, and now had to fill myself again in order not to collapse like a cardboard box. An angel had for a tiny moment gone through me and with its radiant aura had shown me the emptiness that was bounded by two glowing points, by my work and by *The Divine Comedy*.

Glowing points, comparable to the little spiral lamp that in my childhood showed me the way to the bathroom. A fading piece of a residue of energy, not worth mentioning. But there were — the angel had showed me that in an incomparable way — still these last sparks. If they didn't catch, then it was over. Then I could have given everything up or had to accept the professorship I had been offered. "How do you hold a brush?" "This is the way you hold a brush!" No, I had to fan the fire — no matter how difficult that was, the spark had to become a flame — with all the power that remained in me, so that cynicism and irony, cold fury, sentimental intelligence, and pathetic pain — which lurked outside to possess me finally like a house standing empty — would find no entry. Left to myself I would have missed the change in my life — the angel had been the great glowing finger that had shown me the place and time.

I had understood. And under my hands something came into being that I had never seen before. Nothing new, and certainly not the new school of landscape painting that my gallery owner hoped for to enliven his salon, accompanied by a new slogan. Anything that originated in the cities was dishonest business. Many of my colleagues were already

76

even flirting with the new fascism to get a few words in. One had discovered the North, the broad expanses of the sea of ice; already ice paintings were cropping up everywhere, the Nordic School was founded, the Ice School, and anyone who didn't know any better moved to Iceland just to escape the South, the South drained empty. Like grasshoppers, they moved from concept to concept, like thieves, now here, now there, when business was booming — then they took off for greener pastures. That also had its ironic aspects, of course, but sadness predominated at the sight of that activity. In my tower, on the other hand, I was sticking to the basics, or so it seemed to me anyway. And the social consequences were also soon discernible.

After only two weeks I was completely out of control. Monsieur Jopin, whom I had asked to get me some wood, was alarmed when he stacked the firewood in the kitchen for me. Apparently he believed my bad conscience had turned me into a hermit. And when I stood facing him, I naturally did not notice how much I had changed outwardly. As always, he was wearing his blue shirt under the black jacket, whereas I had on a spotted pullover, dirty slippers, and torn pants, from which my knees were peering. I hardly ever shaved and seldom bathed because I believed I had no time for such formalities. In addition to the paintings, I still had to manage *The Divine Comedy*, which grew into the dominating project of my evening hours. I worked on it at least four hours daily and in the coming weeks, when the days became shorter, would work even longer. Besides, I had an extensive reading program to complete, for which I had reserved the early morning hours when it was still too dark for the easel. The book I was devouring at the time was entitled *Labyrinth and Cave*. "There can be only one outcome," I had written in red paint on the endpaper.

15

Nevertheless, the attention strained me to the breaking point. I felt increasingly how the deep concentration, with which I mistrustfully watched the changing paths of color on the canvas, gave way to a sluggishness, a tugging languor that rose from an abyss inaccessible to me and drained the energies of my eye. At first I thought that only my accumulated observation was becoming diluted, that my memory was abating, and that I had to go out again into nature to check the colors and recharge the batteries of my eyes, but when I followed this conjecture and rambled in rubber boots through the landscape, it dawned on me that this phase of painting was gone. The mysterious attraction was no longer operating. The fields were without a comprehensible expression. I had lost my purity, absolute purity and steadfastness. Instead, a distracted waiting mingled with the knowledge of weakness. The loamy colors escaped examination, the blue black mass of the evergreen forests remained only briefly on my retina.

Soon I was dawdling around aimlessly and staring unremittingly into the region, a woeful creator whose imagination failed him from the pure force of production. Nor was I able to capture impressions by writing them in my notebook or to compress them into sketches that I could work out later. The longer I succumbed to my meandering, the farther away I wandered from my goal, and sometimes fear overcame me, fear of never again being able to step up to my pictures.

One small lake, which had formed beyond the western hills in a fold of earth, attracted me. I could not explain why this slate gray water, which patiently reflected the heavy masses of clouds at its center and the dark clusters of trees along its overgrown banks, gripped my attention more strongly than did the clear lines of waving fields that dominated my paintings, since my readiness to expose myself to the bizarre features of the landscape was not especially developed.

Neoromantic enthusiasms that decorated the walls of galleries everywhere were foreign to me. All the finds from exotic lands that were signed unfinished produced nausea in me. Spores, arranged in geometric patterns and given the breath of life by visitors interested in art as ecology, I found ridiculous, especially when a cultural theory sent forth tendrils about those miserable demonstrations, a theory whose paltriness exceeded its incentive. And now I found myself fascinated by nature, by thicket and swamp, by a small pond whose surface seemed almost impervious, like a skin that I pummeled again and again with stones to destroy the unbearable illusion.

A sweet odor of decay rose or hung over the motionless water, just as everything gave the impression of having been brought to a standstill. I had to force my way through seemingly impenetrable thorns, slithered over slippery pine needles that had kept their moistness under the thick canopy, held on fast to the wet ferns that were covered with slimy, white snail trails, and finally stood deeply enraptured

80

and impressed in front of the viscous roundness of putrefying water, as though, like Livingston, I had been the first to discover the Great Fountain in the middle of the primeval forest, the heart of this region.

I sat down on a water-gnawed tree trunk that seemed shackled by ivy and other creepers and watched the frogs diving slowly into the turbidness. On the opposite side, bushes formed a bright vault that contrasted with the darker green of the evergreens and later, in the departing light, when the lake had become black as lacquer, they melted into the darkness. When the shadows became thicker and the play of light trickled away, I set out on my slick return path through the woods, which smelled like resin and dampness, and stepped from the dark corridor back into the brighter openness of the fields, reaching the house again in the last shimmer of daylight.

After these excursions, which made great demands on my senses, any thought of painting was out of the question, and for that reason I swore to avoid such diversions in the future. But the next day, as soon as I had set myself up in front of the easel, I was again drawn into the coldness of the forest, to the blue gray eye of the lake, to the fine tints of the trees that crowded onto its shore. Something clutched me and prevented me from attending to my work. Standing in front of the easel, I saw myself entangled in minutiae and details that disturbed and destroyed the grand construction. Thought and calculation stopped guiding my hand completely; I felt only marginally responsible for the events that dominated me.

Faintheartedly I recognized the weaknesses from which

my pictures suffered — the blunt familiarity of form, the still-decorative antics that prevented them from becoming part of my redemption, from becoming the new pictures of nature that I had dreamed of. I had to scrape off refracted pink, ultramarine mixed with white that was supposed to give stones strength; even the sky came to grief, because the earth no longer could capture its light. Finally I scraped off even the ash-colored background, which suddenly seemed to me like pious mysticism — ashen light, hypocrisy, and affectation. These pictures rested on a false foundation.

"Begin to cry and to complain about the mountains. . . . From the birds in the air to the beasts of the field, everything has fled, vanished." But no complaint helped, I had to start all over again to rouse bird and beast to return.

16

In my world there was no longer a place for the everyday. Occasionally I turned the television set on to have some companionship, but immediately turned it off again. The triumph of a lack of talent was played out for me, in black and white, on all three channels, through which the stupidity of the visible increased in validity. Here they broadcast even the old German detective series that long ago were prohibited in Germany, such as *Derrick* and *The Old Man*, so that I had the horrible pleasure once again of looking into the eyes of Horst Tappert, which were padded by heavy tear sacs. At home one could admire this flowering of performance art only in border areas, where GDR television could be received. Be received! Obviously, Detective Derrick was received in all of Europe, Derrick *was* Europe.

A hundred years ago, if you asked a person at random on the street in St. Petersburg or Brest what Europe was, you would have heard something about European culture, about courtesy, about melancholy, but today only about Derrick. What Napoleon had not accomplished, Horst Tappert accomplishes effortlessly in the blink of an eye. I hope that he will not be torn apart one day by his Doberman like Horst Köpcke, for then Europe would be finished, a blank screen, sadness in all Europe. Then Horst Bangemann in Brussels could pack it up, and Horst Kohl would have to return to Oggersheim. But the guy was still alive. He could solve any crime in forty-five minutes, whereas the French detectives who were after Fat Peter obviously needed months.

And finally, one night when, worn out by *Paradise* and rhymes I could not find, I again turned on the European lunacy, I saw that there was a revolution in Germany. I saw the streets through which I had walked holding my grandfather's hand, the bombed houses, now with makeshift repairs, the Old Market in Leipzig, where in the summer of 1952, a few months before his death, we had eaten ice cream, bought from a seller with a top hat who had two monkeys that accepted feather-light coins, tested their resistance to a bite, and then put them in a little basket. When the stationery shop came into view, on the street that leads from the Old Market to the Thomas Church, I had to turn it off, because tears gushed from my eyes. "Here Herr Grüner waits on you," a sign had said, and Herr Grüner had sold me the first box of paints in my life, a black tin box of paints from Czechoslovakia that I still have today.

I pulled on my rubber boots and walked restlessly across the nocturnal fields, called out the news to the ducks and the owls that, with throaty sounds, enlivened the darkness, and only at dawn returned to the tower. Much to my surprise it stood untouched and in quiet repose in the pale light of the early-fall day, as though nothing had happened.

The last line of my external degeneration had been crossed when one day one of my teeth fell out, top front in the middle. I looked at it as though it were something that came from another world and finally laid it on the palette, where soon it was covered with an agglomeration of color. I am falling apart. If it continues at this pace, I will soon be able to define myself by my parts. The core is melting and falling off in pieces. Certainly I was no coward faced with life, no evader, but the lack of that last line was becoming more noticeable every day. Even Monsieur Pierre, who as a café owner had to be accustomed to all kinds of things and wasn't exactly all there, much less a beauty, made a face when I ordered my pastis toothlessly.

Now I drove into the city only once a week. In Agen I had bought a sandy colored Citroën from a used-car dealer. It could not replace the old one, of course, but as a substitute did its job. The ambassador has been ordered back home, but the first deputy councillor is at your service.

Home? Where was that? The place where the puritanical idealism imposed by the state was removed?

I bought great stores of noodles, processed milk, and all sorts of canned goods that always had to last for a week. If not, then I starved. That did my body good — soon it had grown very thin, which again eased my standing in front of the easel. I drank a lot. Water and wine. Since in this part of Europe you could not return the bottles, I had big problems with my trash. I did not want to throw the empty bottles into Monsieur Jopin's trash container — in general, I wanted to see him as little as possible. We said hello at a distance, respectfully, and he was obviously glad not to have to look at me close up. One day I put all the bottles into the car, which was soon filled up to the roof, and set out looking for a trash dump. I did not find one. It rained like crazy, and I sat in the stinking car, puddles of wine on the floor, but not a trash can far or near.

When I was just about to stuff the first bottles into the wastebasket at a bus-stop shelter, I heard a honk behind me. A bus, completely filled with patients from a nearby hospital who were being driven to Sunday mass. Poor devils, every one deranged, who with mild faces turned were looking through the windows and obviously talking with one another about the sight of the man with the bottles. They would straightway be taken to see God, a powerless God, who did not understand their language. A few years ago they were kept at home, now they were hidden away in a special clinic that was situated very near me in a woods. Anyone who has enough money can hide his child away. A woman left the bus; she probably thought nothing of Christian mercy. I jumped in my car, and in my excitement stepped on the gas so hard that the vehicle hopped and the bottles rolled between my feet.

Even in the county seat there were suburbs where people lived in prefabricated houses because they could no longer stand life in the beautiful but crumbling and cold city houses. One of those yellow monstrosities looked abandoned and had a beautiful, big, black trash container at its door. I drove up and down the street in the streaming rain three times to be certain that no one was watching me, then I stopped in front of the house and began to unload my bottles. A frightful noise erupted, which was unavoidable. And suddenly a jalousie shot up, a window opened, and the owner of the dairy store, from whom I had bought hundreds of bottles of milk, roared at me, in a bellowing language that lacked all humor. He came running into the yard in his pajamas, screaming. The last thing I needed was for him to scream murderer or call the police.

Anyway, he forced me in the streaming rain to pick my bottles out of his trash can, a repugnant task because the container was almost six feet deep. In front of his angry eyes I had to climb in, pull each bottle individually out of the wet garbage, and hand them to the owner of the dairy store, who set them down on the ground. He threw some bottles right past my head because he himself had drunk them dry.

"Those are mine," he said, while the shards flew past my body.

Anyway, when all the bottles were stowed away in my car, he showed me the way to the garbage dump, but I was so infuriated by his demeaning treatment that on the way there I tossed a great many of the bottles out the window into the ditch.

17

At morning the wind, which had afflicted the house all night long with lashing blows, had died down. At first it had been only a slight breeze, which once in a while softly rattled a window shutter or sometimes the door, as though to test its mounting strength; then it rustled fiercely in the fireplace, stirring the white ashes. Later, when I looked out the window, I saw the wind rummaging through the hedge and startling the birds. A hazy moon tried with its last strength to break through the speeding clouds, until I suddenly was staring into an ink black night that towered up like a wall about the narrow wedge of light.

> *Returns to his house and to and fro complains,*
> > *Like a starved wretch who knows not what to do,*
> > *Then again comes out and his hope regains,*
> *Seeing what the world has changed its face into*
> > *So briefly.*

I had read in the twenty-fourth canto of *Purgatorio* and compared the translations because certain passages were more and more incomprehensible to me, but with a rising wind, which had begun like a rolling swell of surf and then had held the wall fast and wouldn't turn loose, persistent reading had become impossible. When hail finally began drumming against the windows, all sense of external living motion left me.

Suddenly I felt alone. For the first time I no longer felt merely abandoned in this secure house, rather forgotten, cut off, dismissed. And no one was there to lift me up on the pinnacle of a cliff and say roughly to me:

> *Now it behooveth lassitude to leave,*
> *. . . for softly on down reclined*
> *Or under coverlet, none can fame achieve.*

Even alcohol no longer helped. The second bottle of red wine had vanished in me without a trace; the feeling of strangling remained.

The wind had clawed itself fast into the walls, into the scruffy stones that began to quiver in its merciless embrace. The lamp shook, the floor boards crackled, everything seemed to adapt to the irregular rhythm of the cold wind. The branches of the tamarisk slapped with furious harassment against the kitchen window; the door withstood the charging exhalation only with difficulty; the whole tower, built as though for eternity, was filled by a deafening roar.

I had become a spectator of a drama that surpassed my horizon, and so it was hard for me to keep an aesthetic attitude. A man of deed ought to be there, someone who leapt over borders and could act, even if only to close the shutters. But just the idea of having to do something about this upheaval of nature crippled my resolution. The book weighed heavily in my hand. Only with difficulty did I bring the cigarette to my lips. I had to lift the wineglass with both hands. Finally the lights went out. Today and tomorrow were of no importance in this situation; the fever of creation had subsided too much from sheer fright to still be an incentive for art.

And at morning the sky was again lustrously bright.

18

Without any warning, I received unexpected help in my
curious situation — to which I owe not only fourteen enormous paintings but also, because of my enemies, the most
agitating disquiet of my life — when one afternoon Monsieur Jopin's daughter appeared at the door. It must have
been a Sunday. Actually, she wanted only to pass on a
written document from the police, which had arrived at the
Jopins' that morning, but she stayed until I had cleaned the
paint off my hands with turpentine, and she willingly
agreed to join me in deciphering the bureaucratic language
of the document. She had learned German at school, which
helped me make some sense out of the confounded phrases
of the document. She had had a downright tragically
tortured expression on her face as she stood at my door in
the half-light, but now, after tea and some bad wine, she
brightened up, and the uncommon misgiving that had
distorted her face seemed to be assuaged. Uneasy about
my peace and quiet, I looked at her surreptitiously from
the side, for I wasn't prepared for a conversation. Had her
father sent her to feel me out? Did she want to find out for
herself?

She was small in stature, stocky, dark. And very slow.
I had always been attracted to slow people who are able
to escape the bustle. Neither hunters nor game. Drowsiness as a permanent refuge. Such people order their lives

differently, better; they can organize themselves more exactly. For them the world does not exist according to causal laws and is not regulated according to their needs and satisfaction.

A heavy knitted pullover stuck out from under her hooded jacket, her feet were in cowboy boots. On the one hand, she annoyed me by her tired, ironic nods whenever I said something against the methods of the French police, and on the other hand, I was close to surrendering to a strong longing to embrace her when, in her slow, awkward German, she tried to explain to me how I should behave in the future. Sitting so catlike at my table, what would she say if, after the completion of the translation, I gave her a lecture about the necessary solitude of the painter, instructions in emptiness, exhaustion, boredom, the precious possessions of the artistic, time-renouncing loner, which, however, he is willing to share for short moments? Would she, in her interpretation, make good use of that, and if so, for whom?

"May I paint you?" I asked.

"Why not," she said.

I got a drawing pad and pencils from the studio, sat her down on a chair next to the fireplace, where I laid two large logs, and handed her *The Divine Comedy* in the translation by the twentieth-century poet.

I sketched until I had caught her provocative repose, caught what was childlike and carefree in her appearance. I stared at her, then I merely looked at her, in the end I had made her so much a part of me that the memory of my hand sufficed to do justice to the form of the reading girl. I had to smile when I noticed, looking up, that she had taken off her pullover and her boots, since she was long since portrayed on the paper without them. Slowly her body emerged from a diffuse background of color, and although with increasing labor I broke every academic rule and in spite of virtuoso artisanship abrogated the laws of perspective with great daring, finally drawings of so rare a charm grew out of the initially vague material that the departure from reality was caught up and imbedded in a larger frame.

Even though throughout many hours she never looked up for long periods of time, or even returned my gaze, still she understood me. No borders, no barriers could restrain that gaze.

At the end of the long sitting — the light of afternoon had faded into the amorphousness of evening — I had finished four drawings, four icons with a nude Madonna, reading a book from which all letters had been removed.

She looked at them a long time, and said slowly, provocatively, "I might look like that sometime. Perhaps one day I will look like that, but then you won't recognize me."

19

Sometimes during those days I was seized by the fear that I might change. The self-drawn circle became tighter; my life threatened to suffocate in the labyrinth of my constructions. Once the police called and asked whether I knew anything new, once Marina was on the phone — that was the whole extent of my conversations. From the distance I saw Monsieur Jopin plowing his field; his daughter, whom I had implored to stop by, never came again. I longed for spoken conversations. The tone of Dante, always lofty, had drained my relationship with reality and delivered me into illusory space. Truth, certainty, perception — all the sturdy columns on which I had erected my artistic structure, perhaps for its part illusory, but surely the last stage of painting that was possible for me — began to crumble, so that my art too was threatened with collapse.

My distance from others had remained the single important constant that enabled me to develop my aesthetic attitude. Now I craved the coarsest gossip, wrangling and jabbering with a woman to give my necessary solitude a comprehensible boundary. Nothing is more exciting for a painter than to wander through the landscapes of the mind alone, but, alas, after the empty, uncultivated surfaces that he can fill with his paints, he steps onto the swampy ground of emotions and compassion, where the lack of general norms doubles and finally allows pictures that owe their torpid enthrallment to color or form to come into being. Kitsch. Imagination is robbed of power and unemployed. What remains is an indolent pondering that achieves expression but never reaches a degree of beauty that would be exemplary. Beauty comes into being through the containment of energies, not through gushing; through gathering into the core, not through the admission of peripherals; through the exclusion of the anecdotal, not through its assimilation; through the elimination of direct sensuality.

I had been accused of intellectual painting — now, because of my confinement, I was well on my way to promoting the general process of disintegration that had befallen art in this disinterested world. My own psychological milieu had deteriorated so much that I did not dare to delay taking a step toward self-communion. Otherwise, my paintings, however beautiful they were in the traditional sense, would no longer meet the demands that I had formulated for myself as a holy, unalterable guiding principle. I had to regain the rigor and the tenacity of principle and accept any form of hermetism, in order not to lose forever the lofty demands that had, in any event, retreated from painting.

And who else should tear me from my dull-witted mental confusion but the unattainable woman with the bony face, who had once bent over me and robbed me of my composure?

20

The middle of November had passed when Herr Scheibe arrived, the sausage manufacturer from Saarbrücken. He had not, as had been arranged, announced himself by telephone, but appeared suddenly, honking in front of my door in his officious Mercedes. He came from Toulouse, where he had taken part in a meeting about laws for purity in European sausage, and was utterly depressed. How could I be the very one to cheer up a sausage manufacturer from the Saarland?

"Just come right on in," I said. "You can complain better in front of the fireplace." Like all Saarlanders, he had everything with him that was required to cheer himself up: schnapps, sausage — German sausage, naturally — and a case of Moselle wine, Luxembourg Elbling, which makes your mouth water. He uttered his complaints in a cheerfully unintelligible form — they really had to do with sausages.

"You won't believe what lies in wait for us after 1992," he said, " — pure chaos." The French and the Belgians, according to his worst premonition, would stuff any kind of scraps into artificial guts, any kind of filth; it was a shame to have to compete with them. With those from the south you knew what awaited their stomachs, but that the French and the Belgians, too, who were a part of the real heart of modern civilization, were about to defile sausage was something he could not understand.

"Anything that has a longish look," he said, and gave an approximate measure with his hands, "can be called sausage in the future. No more discussion about content, only form is of interest. If the form looks like sausage, you can sell the form as sausage," he yelled with excited scorn and grabbed a tube of paint: "That, too — a sausage. Who can eat that?"

I did not know how to answer. Traditions centuries long were going down the drain because the French and the Belgians did not want to comply with the purity regulations and confused form with content — the old aesthetics song and dance. The almost hour-long complaint of the sausage maker, which in its substance was not unlike a modern staged debate, ended then with a question that this time, as he said, he wanted to ask as friend to friend:

"What ought I to advise my children? Should they get into the sausage business, sign on for sausage, with these prospects?" His daughter, Petra, was already studying German literature in Munich, a more than unpromising affair, as he confided to me frankly. She was writing her dissertation on Wieland's dramas, which it seemed were unreadable, abstract nonsense. His son was undecided; sausage did not attract him to the extent necessary for him to have a say in the European market.

"He has a shy nature, has no passion for sausage, not for its content, not for the way it looks. What do you say?"

"Hard to give advice," I said dejectedly. "But inheriting a sausage factory is not to be sneezed at. And if your sausage one day becomes the purest sausage in Europe, then your son will be making a unique product. You shouldn't underestimate that! A unique sausage product. And if he goes bankrupt, then he'll still have your paintings," I added, to change to more familiar ground.

"Yes, the paintings," he said, "he understands them even less. The paintings must be taken to a place of safety from him, really. He hates my collection. In that he's like his mother. Damned genes, you're never certain of transmitting the right ones. Either I'll get a little museum," he said, "or I've got to outlive my family. But the Saarland is poor and my demands are high. They'd have to change the name of the municipal museum to the Scheibe Museum, then I'll give them my paintings. But only then. With the money that I earned with my first sausages I bought Beckmann, two pieces, medium size. And when the Lyons factory went into production and the machinery was paid for, I continued with Klee. Three Klees, two large Pechsteins, two Kirchners, a wonderful Müller, which everybody envies me for, four first-class paintings by Gabriele Münter, and so on. And with the sausage spread, which by the way is much better than the spread from Westphalia, much spicier — though it hasn't yet gotten around much, unfortunately — I bought out the Saarland, everything that has status and a name where we live. For every dozen feet of sausage, a painting. Someday the people will open up their eyes! The Saarland is underestimated, as far as art is concerned. Everyone is falling for the Cologne tripe, nobody has come to Saarbrücken. Some day that'll change," he said, "and everyone will have to come to me, to the Scheibe Museum."

I liked him and his boundless patriotism. And whenever did a sausage maker-collector travel to Grazimis to see an artist at work? Besides, his tale relaxed me. I could really feel the spasms dissolving in my back. The sun had not quite reached noon, and already we had drained the third bottle of Elbling and only five fingers of schnapps remained in the bottle. Now and then one of us got up and went to the door to pee; I kept putting on the brittle elm logs that Monsieur Jopin had brought me. All the elms in this region were sick, they were dying, and the wood disintegrated in no time. And then the telephone rang.

I knew immediately who would be calling. Yes, I was so sure that at first I didn't want to pick up the receiver.

"The telephone," said Herr Scheibe. "It's ringing."

It was she. "How are you?" she asked "Are you mad at me?"

"No," I said.

"Do you have company?"

"Yes."

"Nice company?"

"Yes."

"Then I'll call later."

That was all.

"Shit," I said, "shit and damnation!"

And Herr Scheibe, the realistic sausage maker, said, "That's always the way it is. When things are congenial, the women call up and check whether you're being good and have carried out the garbage. It looks like a garbage dump

102

around here," he added cheerfully. "This trash is fantastic. Art and trash, that secret is still waiting to be discovered."

"What's that?" I asked.

"I mean that art and trash, disorder, filth, what you see here, somehow or other do belong together. Have a repercussion on mankind, like beauty. Don't they? Could you paint your pictures in my villa in Saarbrücken? With my wife around? Hard to believe."

He had again instinctively hooked his theme, began to talk at once about the purity regulation, meanwhile eating Lyon sausage voraciously with a knife. "Like my grandfather," he said, "who tested every individual sausage with his finger," and then suddenly was so drunk that in the middle of a sentence he stopped talking.

I hope he doesn't choke, I thought, because his head had fallen onto his chest and alarming sounds came out of his mouth, a twittering rattle that quit, beginning again with a popping explosion. A dead German in the present situation would have been too much of a good thing. I removed the knife with the pure Lyon sausage from his hand, laid his arm about my shoulders, and, murmuring soothing words as though to a sick child, dragged him up the stairs to my bed. I had to stand there bent over because his arm wouldn't let go of my head, but since my back hurt so hellishly, I just dropped down on him and then rolled off, so that both of us ended up lying next to one another. It wasn't exactly congenial, to use one of his favorite words, but it was all right. His rattling snore became regular and was transposed into a kind of gloomy melody that had such a somnolent effect that I finally surrendered to it.

21

Herr Scheibe was the first to wake up and awakened me. He felt terrible, and he didn't know where he was and how he had gotten there. "Did something happen?" he asked me "Did I hurt you?"

"No," I said. "Everything's okay."

We lay there irresolutely and stared into the darkness.

"Do you have lights in the house?" he asked.

I turned on a tall floor lamp, which immersed the chaos around us in a friendly light.

"Do you know *The Divine Comedy*?" I asked him.

He hadn't read it. Under the lamp lay the scholar's translation, which I picked up and opened at random.

"I'll read you a couple of pages. They'll calm you down."

"Let's get a bit comfortable first," he said. He took the crumpled pillow and shook it, laid the fur coverlet carefully over both of us, and crossed his arms on top of it.

I read him canto twenty-eight, the one for which I had already done a few sketches:

> *Who even in words untrammeled, though 'twere told*
> > *Over and over, could tell full the tale*
> > *Of blood and wounds before me now unrolled?*
> *Truly there is no tongue that could avail,*
> > *Seeing that our speech and memory are small*

And for so great a comprehension fail.
Nay, were it possible to assemble all
　　Who of old upon Apulia's fated soil
　　Wailed their spilt blood and friendless burial,
Wrought by the Trojans, or in that long moil
　　Of war which heaped, as Livy writes nor errs,
　　Of Roman rings so marvelous a spoil,
With those who, Robert Guiscard's serried spears
　　Defying, met great hurt and sore distress,
　　And those whose bones the plough still disinters
At Ceperano, where their faithlessness
　　The Apulians proved, and Tagliacozzo, where
　　The aged Erard conquered weaponless;
And one should make his riddled carcass bare
And yet another show his limbs cut off; yet shapes
　　Of fouler fashion in the Ninth Chasm were.
A cask that has lost side- or mid-piece gapes
　　Less wide than one I saw, chopped from the chin
　　Down to that part wherefrom the wind escapes.
The bowels trailed, dropping his legs between;
　　The pluck appeared, the sorry pouch and vent
　　That turns to dung all it has swallowed in.
While gazing on him I stood all intent,
　　He eyed me, and with his hands opened his breast,
　　Saying: "Now see how I myself have rent.
How is Mahomet maimed, thou canst attest.
　　Before me Ali, weeping tear on tear,
　　Goes with face cloven apart from chin to crest.
And all the others whom thou seëst here

> Were, alive, sowers of schism and of discord,
> And therefore in this wise they were cloven sheer.
> There is a devil behind us who hath scored
> His mark on us, and brings each of this crew
> Again to the edge of his most cruel sword
> When the forlorn road we have circled through;
> For all our wounds are healed of blood and bruise
> Ere any of us before him comes anew.
> But who art thou who on the crag dost muse,
> Haply to postpone thine apportioned pain,
> Whatever confessed sins thy soul accuse?"
> "Death comes not yet to him, nor guilty stain,"
> Replied my Master, "chastisement to wreak . . ."

Now he had really fallen asleep. He looked like a pastor because the blanket covered his suit so far that only the lapels and the white collar of his shirt could be seen.

I got up quietly and went down to the kitchen, made some tea, and sat down at the table. Herr Scheibe had stolen my day away. I had to make up for it by working at night.

22

After a sleepless night with and for Dante, I must have gone to sleep at morning on the kitchen table, my head on my arms.

Herr Scheibe had tidied up to the point of uninhabitability. The adjoining room had been transformed back into the salon that I had entered for the first time six months ago. Books were standing on the chest, according to their height, so that *Cave Strolls* had to put up with being neighbor to Zehren's *Testament of the Stars*, which for its part snuggled up to the poet's translations of Dante, prevented from falling by empty pastis bottles. My little *Library of Bats* was at the end. During the summer it had been my advisor when my tower was circled by whole swarms of those nocturnal bloodsuckers, which after long research I was able to identify as Mediterranean horseshoe-nose bats. Now they had swarmed off to their winter quarters, where in the darkness they awaited their hour.

Quite well revived, with rosy cheeks, Herr Scheibe came down the stairs in his wrinkled suit with a small basket of trash, broom in hand. "You just have to get a tooth implanted," he called out to crumpled-up me. "Then order will be restored."

While I was making coffee, he happily cleaned the kitchen, threw the trash into cardboard boxes that he set out in front of the door, and in all earnestness began to sprinkle water in the kitchen, which he spread in broad streaks with the broom.

"After the prologue comes art," he said cheerfully out of the blue. "Now I want to see what you've painted."

"First a stroll," I begged, stricken. "The transition is too abrupt."

I gave him some rubber boots, into which he stuffed his pants legs as though into a sausage, put a straw hat on his head, and pushed him out the door into the pale morning sun that struggled behind vitreous veils of fog. We walked in the direction of Condom, toward the sun, past the old Château de Laroche, whose gray window shutters were tightly closed. A rabbit ran across our path; crows with clay-covered feet strutted across the fields like sullen head-waiters.

I explained the soils, the sequence of crops, the irrigation to him. At a small woods, from which the bare branches of dying elms projected, I showed him the place where in the past week a farmer had fatally shot a mush-room hunter who, in spite of repeated warnings, was not willing to stop his activity. I had to mention that incident because it had relieved my own situation, at least in part. According to Monsieur Jopin, that murder had been at least more excusable than the murder of the policeman because it remained in the family, so to speak. A Frenchman had shot a Frenchman to death for more or less good, or at least understandable, reasons.

"Dangerous region," said Herr Scheibe, to whose shoe soles the clay stuck in thick clumps. "If you can't run, you're gonna die." He wanted to go back to the house. The countryside had become ghastly to him, a field of graves.

"Maybe they're thinking we're mushroom criminals, too," he whispered, when two men approached us across the fields. "Just keep your hands in plain sight."

It was the detective and a man from the cooperative, who politely introduced themselves.

"I'm Scheibe," said Herr Scheibe, "from Saarbrücken."

"What about the missing car?" asked the detective, "Don't forget to call us."

We looked like scarecrows. Herr Scheibe, especially, in his wrinkled suit, had a heavily shopworn look.

"What about the murderer?" I asked. "Still no trace?"

We turned around — I, too, had lost my urge to hike. On the way back I told my companion the whole story. "Good God!" was his only comment. "Good God! Now it's a matter of staying cool." He seemed to have no antenna for the obnoxiousness of the situation, or in his banditlike outfit he enjoyed being seen with a suspect in the vicinity of the scene of the crime.

Toward noontime, when the light was best, I showed him the paintings. He sat in a wicker chair, a bottle of Elbling under his arm. I hauled out canvas after canvas and set them up before him.

"Good God!" he said again. "If my wife were to see that, she'd drop dead."

He bought all my sketches for the paintings that were finished and paid me with a thick book of traveler's checks.

"That covers everything," said Herr Scheibe, and stowed the large-formatted portfolios in his Mercedes, which we had to clean out for that purpose. A rumpled bundle of picture magazines stayed in the tower, his wife's daily reading matter, as Herr Scheibe put it.

"For God's sake, don't show her the drawings," I said. "She'll really keel over dead."

The farewell was touching. The wrinkled, red-faced man held my hand in both of his own, searched for words.

"I'm Ludwig," he said finally. "If you want, you can call me Ludwig. These two days in your tower were the most beautiful days of my life. Good-bye."

We embraced like two men who share a dangerous secret, and I wondered how this enthusiastic astonishment had snuck into that Saarland sausage manufacturer and got stuck there.

"Good-bye, Ludwig," I said. "We'll see one another at the opening of the exhibition of the Four Seasons." And he was already driving away, past the bowling green covered with damp leaves, down the road to the highway, incessantly honking and waving his arms. My last friend had left me.

The house was empty and in an uncanny way clean, as though other people had just been living in it. I walked on tiptoes, not like a painter of enormous pictures, took my thick-rimmed cup out of the sink almost apologetically, filled it cautiously with coffee, slowly stirred sugar into it and, leaning on the kitchen table, drank in tiny, reflective sips. After the turbulent hours with Scheibe, finally a slackening had come again. The walk had already prepared for it, looking at the paintings had ushered it in.

I could hardly imagine living in the city. It wasn't the bustle that scared me, but the language of the city, the shameless and smart-assed prattle. Nothing in the world is more horrible than art talk, serious art babble. I envied musicians their quiet space, into which they could plunge; writers, who wrote on a book for years with the highest concentration, apart and undisturbed, duty bound only to the purity of the word; poets, who could sit in Worms or Fürstenfeldbruck over their wordcraft without having to take part in art fairs and who especially had serious co-thinkers among their colleagues. Among writers I had never heard any unending, digressing, idle talk about publishing houses, weekend editions, and money such as went on in our circles of painters about galleries, Tuscan villas, and crooked museum directors. And what in our case led to crippling gossip was elevated in theirs, to the loftiest heights, as unconstrained conversation.

"Never again," I said out loud to my cup, which snuggled warmly and amiably in my hands. "No visitors ever again! Not by angels, not by sausage makers, not by detectives. My work shall be completed in peace; it shall unfold in quiet."

Art, fine art, had for a long time now amounted to nothing for clear-eyed fantasts and beguiling utopians, for a group touched by the improbable, for a group touched by a creation separated from the world, a group that had confirmed strict rules in order to celebrate their transgression as an adventure. No longer valid were the accomplishments of the abysmal melancholics who conjured up the mirror of reason and of beauty from nothing but paint and, with that, forced powerful resistance to the pitiable sentimentalities of the moderns. They had disappeared because their art was not in demand. Perhaps the idea of painting was still valid, but for a long time now not its realization. But that is what it was all about, the realization of space that noted absence, the no-longer-retrievable loss. That was not lamented by all the lawyers, doctors, and tax advisors, who expected neither beauty nor bewilderment from the millions upon millions of wretched daubs on their walls. They wanted peace from their art — that's what they paid for. That's how I made my living.

I really had to be careful not to become sentimental myself. I certainly could not let the broad stream of honest affection that swept through me when I thought of my drawings, which were traveling in Ludwig's Mercedes through the French province, empty into the broad bed of pitiable sentimentalities that would necessarily destroy every true picture of the absence of the world.

Every picture, every optic whirlpool, every visionary space, every one of the colors in my painting should be a systematization of vanished beauty, an obituary, a compiled, honest obituary, and afterward a powerful, abiding silence should prevail.

I pulled over the pile of magazines that Scheibe had described as being his wife's reference library and leafed through them. What kind of strange tribe was it that was described and presented in those pictures? Were those Germans, Europeans, civilized people? Who, except for Scheibe's wife, read those stories about a countess who had gotten herself a motorcycle, or about a female tennis player whose diffuse love was directed at stuffed toy animals, all portrayed in color? Who was so fascinated by the bad behavior, by the bad taste of others? What kind of people were they, who furnished every one of those vacuous pictures with a caption?

"The Countess of Sachsen-Weimar," it said under the photograph of a skinny blond woman, "at the private exhibition of the painter Carlucci." The painter was not to be seen, and no picture by him either, only an anorexic woman. "General Consul Pappas," a fat man, bent over the ring-covered hand of an ugly blond woman, "greets Ilse von Ansberg, the fashion queen of Schweinfurt." And they all collected art. "I love pines," the countess who had acquired the Honda was quoted, "art and riding motorcycles are the greatest, absolutely super." Dead birds were shown too, which in the caption were described as dead birds, and beside it a politician wrote that something had to be done about the dying off of birds.

It was depressing to leaf through the magazines, deeply disturbing, because I could imagine neither the people who were depicted there nor those who looked at the people depicted there and from that reached conclusions about their lives. And all of them collected something that was still called art, and from it the elevation of the human spirit was to be expected. So all of these weird, blond noblewomen were running around with elevated spirits. Politicians spoke out, who in all seriousness demanded even more art. Even a special museum for Nazi art was proposed because, in comparison to its significance, Nazi art received too little notice in the general offering of art. Also, Neo-Nazi art should be collected more vigorously so that comparisons between Old Nazi and Neo-Nazi art would be possible. It was revolting. Even the concept of art itself was called into question in these magazines.

"For a long time now we've no longer known what we're doing," said a colleague of mine, who was depicted in front of his estate in Tuscany, "but that has nothing to do with art in the usual sense." It was the painter who had proposed me for a professorship; I knew him well, and his pictures, too, which were hanging in all the museums.

A professor of sociology was pictured, who could neither read nor write. "The Illiterate," it said under the picture. The text explained how the man had managed to keep his professorship, and an interview offered, as they say, further background information. "I just pretended to be writing," the Würzburg sociologist was quoted as saying. "In reality I only scribbled, sometimes up and away from the line, sometimes downward; my assistant made that out and wrote a clean copy, then it was printed. Since I can't read, I accept no responsibility for the text, only the fees." And the lectures? "I always just talked about what I think about this society, and that went over well. Traffic sociology, e.g., too many automobiles, no parking places — that interested the young people, and politics, too." Because he had already been a full professor in Würzburg for twenty years, they couldn't throw him out. On the contrary, the minister of education personally promised him a reader and a clerk. "We can't put such an experienced scholar and a pedagogue so beloved by all to the sword just because he can't read or write," the minister of education had said, beneath whose photograph the statement was repeated a bit differently from its wording in the text: "We can't terminate from

116

service to the state everyone who can't read or write. On the contrary, we must help those people, integrate them, learn from them." In the future he wanted to fill many more empty positions with illiterates because they were fresh, not yet exhausted as writers, not yet read. It was horrible. The Würzburg professor of sociology had even given "painting" as his hobby. Not many words are necessary there. Disgusting. And to beat all, in Würzburg, under the eyes of Tiepolo.

I was about to get up and consign the pile of magazines to the indifferent fire when I suddenly saw Fat Peter. No doubt, it was he. I recognized him by the funny chain that he wore over his shirt also in the photograph. He was sitting in the first row of the Olympic Stadium in Munich listening to a rock band, the latest rage from America. A social event of the first order that was documented extensively on the following four pages.

All of my new acquaintances were pictured: the motorcycle countess wearing a dirndl, but almost bare on top; also two of my colleagues who had specialized in body art ogling the cleavage of the Countess of Sachsen-Weimar, as though something could be gained there for art appreciation and educational methodology. And in the midst of all this splendor, my Fat Peter, the suspected murderer of the Toulouse policeman.

It was like a slap in the face because I was not at all prepared for this appearance. The caption was of no help to me either. Every other one of the pictured persons had a name and played a respectful role in the social life of the city, from the party king, Everding, a chubby dwarf who was standing in the middle of almost every photograph, to the beauty queen — only Fat Peter had been left nameless. Again, in the caption for another photograph, where he was depicted in a group that was connected with a Munich poet and boxer dressed in leather, his name was not given. Perhaps no one really knew him. Perhaps he always simply took an empty seat in the first row, fat and seemingly watching, or joined groups that were discussing generally interesting problems such as boxing and literature, and then went later to his hotel to separate the false Cartier watches from the genuine ones.

There were always people who were unknown, had no names.

I called up a friend in Munich, a pharmacist by trade, who worked as an editor, gave him the name of the magazine, the page, the picture, and asked him to find out the name and address of the nameless man.

"My life depends on it, my good fortune, and my car," I told him. He laughed because he understood none of it, but promised to call me back.

"How's art?" he asked in closing.

"When you see the new pictures, you'll drop dead," I said, and hung up.

Every picture should be an obituary that shamed the friends of art and silenced them.

23

I was weary. The light was again decreasing, becoming thinner. A magpie was practicing dives in front of the window, all the while squawking like a child. The raven returns from the funeral, the magpie shows half mourning, I had once read.

A child. A pain. A deceptive perspective. Images from memory, last stage. Perhaps I should go to sleep, even if I were to wake up again in the middle of the night. Independent from clock time, my day's labor was ended — it no longer needed divisions of time. After the phase of unabashed work, I had obviously glided into another condition that managed without firm rules and regulations, without the on-and-off of concentration and exhaustion. "May it endure," I said solemnly into the room, and hoped that my wish would remain valid as a motto for December.

The telephone rang. The telephone always rings, even in a wilderness.

"What did you find out?" I asked into the mouthpiece, in the assumption that the pharmacist had discovered something.

"That you're a painter," said the strange woman.

"Oh, that, too," I said. "Our love suffers when you don't occasionally stop by. You probably wouldn't even recognize me anymore."

"Did you lose a tooth?" she asked.

How did she know that? Why did this voice persecute me, instead of leaving me in peace? Peace in a collective sense — I wanted peace, not torture. Voices are the most common means of torture that mankind can endure, and particularly evasive voices, flattering but evasive voices.

"When can I finally use my car again?" I asked.

"Is it so urgent?" she retorted. "Don't you like your new car?"

It was hopeless.

"I long for you, that's all," I said, and hung up. Stupid snout. Tomorrow I'll go to the police and report the theft of the car, then they'll start a search at whose end maybe I'll see the woman again in the courtroom. Where is she? Where has she hidden herself? What is she doing at this moment, now that I've hung up the receiver? Is she furious, content, cheerful? Is a man sitting near her who's following the comedy laughing?

In the mail, which lay still unopened on the table, was a letter from an art magazine whose chief editor asked me fervently for a contribution, to shed light on the undergrowth of the contemporary art scene. Now they came crawling. For years these youngsters with their high-gloss pages had cut me, now they themselves did not know what was going on.

"Pursuant to the law according to which it appeared on the scene, Western civilization has learned nothing from its art. It has not understood the offerings that art contains — for knowledge, for life, for associating with creation — and has drawn no consequences from it. The result now comes to light undisguised. In the most important industrial nations, under the sign of neoconservatism, a hierarchical substitution has taken place that favors big money especially. At the same time a pan-social mentality has been established in which excessive consumption for all has become the sense-determinant way of life. If, parallel to that, contemporary art remains so beloved and in demand, then this has completely ambivalent aspects."

Why didn't he just reprint his letter, why should I even comment on this banal monstrosity that he had erected for me in his dainty handwriting? Basically this lowlife was interested in neither truth nor art, rather exclusively in ideology, in their ideology, and the letter, which moved hand over hand for many pages from concept to concept, was the best example of false consciousness, delusion, and prohibition of thought. Specialists in exposé. It was a matter of exclusion, and I, for years ostracized, was supposed to play policeman: this far and no farther.

In this conspiratorial request to put myself at their disposal with clarifying words in the rescue of the autonomy of art, which was in danger in the face of its absolute salability, the choice of my person was not of interest — in an emergency one expects all kinds of things from outsiders — but rather the circumstance that the editors of this magazine, which generally served up a judgment or a final decision every month, had apparently lost their orientation in a minefield they had themselves laid. One false step and they would be blown up. Now I was to help them achieve self-elucidation, bringing what was timeless and invisible into harmony.

Why, anyway? Why, precisely, should I deliver a program so that, from the misery they had brought on themselves in the eighties with their repulsive dazzling pretentiousness, they might find a path whose appellation would be somewhat more enduring than the concepts they had given themselves in the recent years of economically successful indolence? "We guarantee you that we won't change a word of your contribution, even if we ourselves and our magazine, which in the past has not always treated you and your work squeamishly, should come into the line of fire in the final summation of your argumentation. We need clarity, the clarity of authority. Please write." And in a postscript the editors had offered to put at my disposal four color pages for paintings of my choice, which I could also use exclusively for my own work.

The bait was set out well, no question; still, I didn't bite. Let these dictators of taste stew in the blind alley of their own bad consciences, I didn't want to be their leader. Could anything still be changed? The weakness of the art market, of course, had something to do with the economic weakness of the times, which could change again, if you firmly believed it, whereas the weakness of argumentation in this request excluded any hope of change: discussion about art — as a painter I had to realize that — had sunk so low that it was no longer in a position to describe the inner measure of art. With a howl of rage that was to meant drive away all the demons that had penetrated my room with this letter, I threw it into the fireplace, where in a trice it lost its voice in the flames blazing up.

Should I keep on painting at all? Before any painting

was done, didn't the prattle about painting have to be silenced, first of all? By saying nothing. Keep your trap shut, clench your teeth, shut your eyes. Only in that way could one outlive the times with dignity.

Outside, it was now dark; a wind let the wooden shutters slap against the outer wall; the flames in the fireplace had almost burned out. It was time something happened, and if nothing occurred, I would have to get myself going in order to escape my void in time.

I looked sternly at the telephone, then at the Dante edition. If the telephone didn't ring, I would have to return to the *Inferno*. "You unimaginative apparatus," I yelled out loud, "get moving," because I had no urge for the *Inferno* and its terrible rhymes. "Say something!"

And it did ring. I let it go on ringing, to test my power of resistance, but my inner tension won out.

It was she again. "Don't hang right up again," she said. "You must learn to rein in your impatience. A painter mustn't be nervous, or else he'll never succeed in anything. Think of your paintings when you speak to me."

In the truest sense of the word, I was speechless, silent, said nothing, but also could not think about my pictures as she wished. "You just have to get out of your tower," she said, "or else you'll forget time, and anyone who wants to paint the seasons must pay exact attention to time."

She made the suggestion that we should meet in Florence, in the city of Dante — that would be good for my avocation. The next morning I should take the train to Toulouse, then the plane to Milan, there a plane to Florence. I would arrive about six in the afternoon, we would meet at Borgo San Lorenzo 4, the key was in the bakery opposite. It would be handed over to me without a question.

"What name?" I asked.

The name was unimportant. They would recognize me at once.

"And when are you coming?" I asked. "If at all?"

"Later," she said, "but early enough. And don't ask too many questions. Questions spoil the game."

Yes, I wanted to go. Wanted to ask my unfinished work to excuse me for a while. Hell, too, could wait:

> As one that is with lust of gain devoured,
>> When comes the time that makes him lose, will rack
>> His thoughts, lamenting all his hope deflowered,
> To such state brought me, in dread of his attack,
>> That restless beast, who by degrees perforce
>> To where the Sun is silent drove me back.

And like someone who does something risky to put his work to the test, I took farewell of my paintings. Perhaps I'll never see them again, I thought, as I pulled every picture under the lamp and tried to impress it exactly on my mind.

The Doomsayer called, but had found out nothing. Not yet; he wanted to keep trying. "Drugs?" he asked, but I didn't know what to answer.

I wanted to inform neither Monsieur Jopin nor the police that I was traveling out of the country. If you have a secret in this translucent world, you can't share it. Above all, not with the police. I packed my bag and set it next to

124

the door, put the studio in order, washed the brushes, stacked up the translated pages of the *Comedy*, and stored them in the kitchen cabinet. Then I went to bed, anxious as a child. I could expect no mercy from this night — the dreams would test me.

24

People in this area go to bed so early that around ten o'clock the square is empty. Through the windows protected by iron screens at the post office, I see the officials lying on their cots; in the butcher shop the sleeping butcher is holding a bloody calf's head in his arms; and in the bank, which I visit to cash a check, the coins welling from the open vault have crushed the employees. So I wander through the city that is empty of cars, empty of people. Only in the darkened bistro is a waiter polishing the counter, whose shine through the window acts like a signal. I am enthralled by this sight and hardly notice how the cold is paralyzing my bones. Through the dirty panes the movements of the man take on a confusing significance that has no relation to his activity. Sometimes I have the impression that my presence is being noticed, because the face of the waiter grimaces, when he looks up; but he makes no effort to speak. Now he extinguishes the light and leaves me all alone in the world. If it weren't for the cold, it would be nice to be alone.

Finally someone puts a coat around my shoulders, a kind of shawl through which I have to stick my head and that presses my arms against my body. I am caught, try to free myself from the encirclement, struggle, scream.

When I woke in terror, a shape was sitting on the edge of my bed, wrapped in a thick pullover. "You're not alone in the world," she said. "You don't have that privilege, even when you scream like that."

It was Monsieur Jopin's daughter, who had come into the tower, God knows how, and held my hand, apparently until I fell asleep again. When at dawn's twilight I lurched into the kitchen to make myself coffee, I saw on the table a note that she had left behind.

"When you come back home after your flight and want to see me, I'll be there."

Back home?

25

The airport at Toulouse invites hijackings. A deep drowsiness had fallen upon the officials who in custom official and police uniforms squinted at my shabby bag and my plastic ID card. No interest in contents or identity. Hardly credible that here, just a few centuries ago, the heretics defied the central authority of the pope. At the Lufthansa counter a weary line of Germans immediately released a feeling of relief in me. You don't have to go back to Germany; nobody knows that you're German.

With a mixture of sympathy and malicious glee, I looked at them, well-dressed ladies and gentlemen, a bit stodgy, probably Airbus co-workers who were looking forward to Christmas, all draped with boxes and packages. Where did this feeling of happiness come from, which I had so often felt before? Why was it, on the other hand, so difficult, so demoralizingly difficult, to imagine oneself a part of the lineage to which one belonged, according to language and origin?

All the planes were late, as usual. Deceleration increases with speed, thank God. You were forced to rest, forced to wait restlessly. We were all waiting, patients for whom there was no cure. With pale faces the passengers slunk through the dismal terminals, got coffee, leafed through newspapers that they threw down carelessly because they evidently knew everything that was in them, had finished reading about all

129

the wars. The battle against the drug Mafia was no longer news, although supposedly every ninth German mark in world trade was involved with drugs. Nothing interesting.

Bild, the illustrated tabloid, had a drawing of a penis on the front page in order to make clear where a surgeon would operate on the chancellor of the Federal Republic. A little arrow pointed to the place involved. Is there another country in the world that enjoys seeing the graphic penis of its chancellor on the front page of the newspaper? Probably not. Probably only Germany — so banal and vacuous, having slid so far down the incline of gobbled-up decadence — was interested in the prostate problems of its chancellor. Repulsive. The horizon of civilization has been abandoned when the chancellor's penis gets onto the front page of the newspaper. I was ashamed. Yes, a feeling of shame and fury rose in me when the lady who was sitting beside me folded the overlarge format so that, with an ironic grin, she could study the article next to the substitute penis. I took the poet's translation of Dante out of my pocket to escape the nightmare that had caught and held me, and after only a few lines I had reached exaltation again, the overpowering loftiness whose moral dimension freed me from all baseness.

> *The day was sinking and the darkling air*
> *Unburdened all the creatures in the world*
> *Of all their cares — and I alone prepare*
> *Myself to take control of plight entwirled,*
> *Of pity, 's well as all of those around*
> *That I will bind into a sense unfurled.*

O Muse — be, O lofty spirit, with me bound!
  O sense of what I saw thee write within thee:
  Here do thou thy patrician tidings sound.

"E io sol uno m'apparecchiava a sostener la guerra sì del cammino e sì de la pietate": the poet had translated "war", the battle between path and pity, with "plight", a word that better expresses hesitation and despondency than *war,* an allusion to the *bellum* of Aeneas. And how beautifully had he translated *"O Muse, o alto ingegno, or m'aiutate"* with "lofty spirit," when all others had preferred "high genius," which is high and exalted only when it gives wings to the spirit. Tears actually came to my eyes as I sat there in the ugly terminal next to the newspaper readers and studied my poet, and I was on the point of reading the descent into Hell eloquently out loud, when the boarding announcement restrained me from that imprudence: the loss of grandeur could not be better demonstrated.

I don't like to fly. Forced sitting troubles me. I don't like the divine perspective, the food, the cold tableware that can be gotten out of the pack only at the risk of your life, the red wine that's always too cold, the sulky faces of the stewardesses who have to force themselves to smile.

The woman sitting next to me, with whom I had begun a conversation only from sheer listlessness and boredom, was going to Asolo to visit the Duse house, *la Casa Luminosa, tranquillo riposo della grande attrice.* She came from Rome and was getting an advanced degree at the University of Toulouse with a work about D'Annunzio and European decadence, about which she reported to me at

131

length and even humbly, as though I were the chief pastor who had to administer the examination.

"Why did Duse, a woman of the world, who had society crawling at her feet, go to Asolo of all places?" she asked me.

"No idea. Perhaps, with D'Annunzio, she wanted to repeat the story of Pietro Bembo and Caterina Cornaro," I said, "the great, the greatest love story in the world, which took place only in letters. True love needs no caresses." She looked at me singularly crushed, as though she were testing whether I was serious. "Apparently all that caressing and openmouthed staring drove love away," I said, "and forever, at that."

A partly obstinate and partly elegant conversation followed this small sentence, during which the woman unflinchingly put a comforting hand on my arm, something that by no means escaped my notice, as though she were about to say: You mustn't think so badly of love; even today love has a lot of nice things to offer; you just have to surrender to it, acquiesce to it. And after an initial aversion I liked her mouselike hand and just waited for her to tap me and call me to order, so that, whenever it lay in the safety of my neighbor's lap for very long, I uttered some senseless sentence or other against love, to lure it forth again, which also promptly occurred.

The high point of this game took place at nine thousand feet over Milan, when the plane flew into a turbulence and the woman, having become uncertain and anxious, trusted her hand to mine, which immediately closed upon it tenderly and tightly, as though it wanted never to let go. Until the

132

bouncy arrival in Milan we remained sitting in this affectionate position, talking about Browning, who — something I didn't know — had likewise been in Asolo. " *'E terra e cielo e colli, valli, alberi, fiori, tutta la esuberante bellezza di Italia mi si affacciava in te,'* " the Italian lady whispered fervently, when with a great jolt, which made the small plane groan, we touched the soil of Italy. I wasn't sure whether I had to read Browning again, too, even though the great love story that bound him with Elizabeth Barrett fascinated me in its unfathomable purity; but with its Anglo-Italian pathos, *Men and Women*, which I had read as a young adult, was not among my best memories.

Hand in hand, soaking with sweat, we entered the terminal; separated briefly before the eyes of the policeman, who inspected us individually for a long time and piercingly; then joined again and finally stood a bit superfluously facing each other, really looking one another in the eye for a long time, for the first time.

"I'm Anna," the graduate student said, and put a calling card in my jacket pocket. "You must visit me in Toulouse."

"At Christmas," I said. "We'll meet on Christmas Eve at the midnight mass in St.-Sernin."

On the trip to Florence, already no longer certain and thoroughly shaken to the core, I took out the card. Dottoressa Anna Bollati. I sniffed at it. It smelled a bit dusty, but not unpleasant. "Anna Bollati, stand by me," I said softly to myself, and fell asleep.

26

The Borgo San Lorenzo lies five minutes from the cathedral and was easy to find. The building in which we were to meet was squeezed in between two shoe shops, whose displays reminded me that I absolutely had to buy some new shoes. It was raining. I went into the bakery, where the key was handed over to me immediately with a matter of course that startled me. I unlocked the door to the building, which was right on the street. A stairway led upward, lit by a naked bulb. It smelled musty and was ice-cold. Cautiously I went up the worn steps and stood before a door left ajar. I knocked and entered. I was in a kitchen to which a bedroom was connected. A bed and a table were the only furniture. On the floor was a record player; a few books, German and Italian, lay next to it, among others *Oblomov* in translation.

Wet as I was, I sat down on the only chair and opened that sacred book: " 'What if now you become tired of this love,' " it began, " 'as you have become tired of books, service to the state, and society? What if you, in the course of time, without a liaison, without another to love, suddenly fall asleep next to me, as you do alone at home on the divan, and my voice is unable to awaken you? What if the swelling of your heart fades away? What if you would prefer not even another woman but a *chalab* . . . ?' "

What is a *chalab*?

" 'Olga, that's impossible!' he interrupted her, insulted, and jerked away from her.

" 'Why impossible?' she asked. 'You say that I'm wrong, that I will love another, but I believe sometimes that you'll simply stop loving me. And what then? How will I justify what I now do? Even if I disregard people and the world, but what shall I say to myself . . . ? That's why even I can't sleep sometimes, but I don't plague you with suppositions about the future because I believe in something better. With me happiness overpowers anxiety. I know how to appreciate it, when your eyes light up when I appear, when you scramble up the hill to look for me, when you leave what you're doing and hurry into the city in the greatest ardor to get me a bouquet or a book, when I see that I make you smile and want you to live. . . . I wait and look for only one thing — happiness, and believe that I've found it. If I'm wrong, if it's true that I'll cry over my error, then at least I feel here' — she put her hand on her heart — 'that I'm not to blame for it; that is, fate didn't intend it, God did not let it happen. But I'm not afraid of future tears; I will not cry in vain: I have bartered something for them. . . . I felt . . . so good!' she added.

" 'Then you shall feel good again!' pleaded Oblomov.

" 'You foresee only dreaming and darkness: happiness doesn't matter to you. . . . That's ingratitude,' she continued. 'That's not love but . . .' "

I was too cold to keep on reading calmly. Besides, a lighted sign, which at short intervals flashed and flooded the room with a flitting blue, bothered me. I stepped to the

136

window and from above looked at the passersby, who hurried through the passageways with big shopping bags.

They're buying the place up in this city of merchants, I thought; when will it stop? They were all well dressed and were buying new clothes. All had shiny shoes and pushed their noses flat on the shoe shop windows.

"Get lost," I yelled against the windowpane. "Take off — the Heavens will devour you."

It's really time for the human race to disappear from the face of the earth, I thought, if they have nothing else to look for here but a pair of shoes and a pullover. They can take the platitudes that they need to live with them, the whole colorful dreariness of their system of compensation will be tossed after them. They ought to just take off. Even philosophers, serious people, should not live here. What do they explain to the shoppers, I wondered? Who listens to them?

Ten years ago I had driven to Florence with my first wife because she wanted to write her doctoral dissertation about Brunelleschi here at the Historical Art Institute: "The Relationship between Ciphers of Measurement and Spatial Forms as a Science of Space." In truth, she had duped me with an infamous comedy, the last act of which had to do with her going to America with a so-called Italian philosopher.

Naturally the Brunelleschi — in whom she wanted to trace a certain satisfaction in the mysticism of numbers beyond the strict rules according to which various chief and subordinate masses were ordered — was not finished, because one baby after the other had to be brought into the world, while the Italian philosopher, a follower of a so-called Theory of Feeble Thought, was busy in the Midwest introducing his demolition of categories to the students of a small college, who considered such nonsense to be *the* ultimate development of Western philosophizing. No, this philosophy had come to an end — if it was one at all and not just Enlightenment-weary stuff-and-nonsense.

There was no doubt about it, if one looked down onto the heads of the people who were standing in front of the shoe shops below me. Any idea of a continuing involvement with great questions bordered on insanity. The nervousness of the sixties had given way to a sugar-sweet harmony; the resistance of thought had melted into diffuse confusion. So now feeble thought, which had conformed absolutely to the taste of the times, avoiding any controlled design, prevailed. Like a dreamer, I looked down from above onto the tangled mass, onto its arbitrary and fruitless structure, which I damned to hell. How long would it be until the world could finally recover from it?

It was almost ten o'clock. Hunger announced itself mightily. Where was the woman who, with such firm resolution, had lured me to this cold Florentine dump? Worriedly I looked at the narrow bed on which our reunion was to have been celebrated, the sad chair, the rickety record player and the miserable records, the photographs, fastened on the wall with drawing pins, one of which depicted the unknown woman and Fat Peter in front of Santa Croce arm in arm. The only thing touching me was dust, which in a downy layer covered everything in this dark, partitioned room. Everything looked worn out, depreciated, vulgar.

I tore a page out of my notebook and wrote the message that I had gone to eat at Alberto's, a bar that I remembered on the other side of the cathedral. There my former wife's present husband had explained to me the adventure of speculating in futures while he probably had played footsie with my wife under the table. "The old way of thought has to be eradicated from the heart of categories," I still hear him saying, but he had erred in the organ, I'm convinced of that even today.

The bar still existed, and even inside, it looked unchanged, only the people eating here seemed to be more prosperous. I had to sit down at a table that was occupied by three other persons, who reluctantly let me join them. The man, who immediately and with exaggerated irony introduced himself, was a professor at a European college, the two women, as was apparently customary in Florence, were art historians, one of them from Munich, as she confided to me at once when I admitted I was German.

I learned that my wife's professor was still around, as was the lady librarian who had helped me back then to get over the bewilderment of my wife's departure. Florence is a village, the art historian from Munich summed up, as she remained sitting when the two others had taken their leave. How did I know my way around so well, I was asked, and I put together a story that sounded confusingly like my own. And it fitted into the picture of this fanciful night that my former wife was visiting Florence, as the woman from Munich told me, because her husband, whom she described as having become the leading thinker of the School of Feeble Thought, had actually tried to obtain a post as philosopher with a lecture the day before about Heidegger and Difference. The only thing missing was that they were not sitting at the next table, I thought, and looking over at me without recognizing me.

I had no idea where I got the composure in my vacuous state to listen to the cozy chatter of the art historian. She talked and talked, as though we had known one another for years, while in thought I traversed sweeping expanses to avoid the pressures that ravaged me. Sometime or other we paid an unwelcome check considering the surroundings and the quality of the pasta, then she took me by the arm, as though I were ailing, and led me out into a sleeping Florence, past all the triumphal structures, which stood dark and wet with rain along our path, until soaked through and weary we stopped before an old building.

"You must be quiet," she whispered excitedly and pushed me through the door and along dark hallways to an apartment that we entered without turning on the light. I struck a bed with my foot and simply let myself fall. I had never felt so alone in the world.

27

The slip of paper from my notebook, which I had laid on the kitchen table the night before, still lay there when toward noon I again entered the apartment on the Borgo San Lorenzo. I checked the page in *Oblomov*, the record on the record player — no one had been there in my absence, no one had noticed my absence. It's nice not to have to follow a specific scheme, but it's unpleasant for someone like me to follow an invisible scheme.

The problems of freedom in cities unfamiliar to us have not been researched. On the one hand, the world gains color; on the other hand, it pales because one cannot assimilate what one sees and experiences. I needed quiet. There was nothing to do, I had only to wait. Waiting makes objects appear more vividly. You become interested suddenly in minutiae, specks of dust, doorknobs, the pattern of the grain on the tabletop. Everything becomes a significant sign that needs clarification. Things force a mode of perception upon you. You yourself become the tool of a power that escapes your own manipulation. In order to elude the wilderness quickly expanding around me, attended by an excessively strong perception of trivialities, I decided to look at nothing more for a while, to notice nothing more. Things should come to me, not the reverse.

So I pulled my chair up to the window, laid cigarettes and matches on the windowsill, and took a seat. The art historian, who had so guilelessly and painfully reminded me of my earlier life, particularly of the time with Brunelleschi, the idol of many years, but also of my former wife and her misdeeds, perhaps committed out of weakness because she was unable to collect her meager energies — and in the end her marriage to the Italian philosopher could not be explained other than by mental infirmity — the art historian, who in my opinion represented the approaching end of European art history, had given me the name of a dentist in the early morning and had also escorted me to him.

After lengthy negotiations and experiments, he had put an artificial tooth in for me, a false thing that anyone who looked at me would have recognized at once as a foreign body. In three days it was to be exchanged for a tooth matching in shade, the result of complicated rhetorical exertions. But nobody looked at me anyway. The artificial tooth radiated an aching pain that soon occupied the entire cavity of my mouth, then my whole head. It was now preparing for a general attack on my body. The pain was beyond comprehension. I grew smaller and smaller under the bell jar of pain, ever so small, ever so insignificant, until it again became bearable.

I sat on my chair and waited. At midday the stream of passersby increased; in the afternoon it grew weaker and threatened to dry up; toward six it increased again. There was no poverty in sight. Poverty was invisible in this street, which was reserved for pedestrians. People walked straight ahead with a rare energy, as though they wanted to replace cars, but their energy seemed sufficient only for moving forward. My toothache concentrated itself at irregular intervals, and sometimes I was almost ready to tear out the foreign object that was in my mouth. Life would be better without the tooth, simpler, freer of pain, and my paintings could come into being without my middle incisor.

It was a long time before I noticed the woman who was sitting on a chair behind a window on the other side of the lane and looking over at me. We're being watched without noticing it, I thought. Someone is always sitting behind a window and recording our movements, and only in a condition of weariness do we become aware of him. Even when many people touch our lives — and recently my life had been quite hectically crossed — we only notice in a moment of complete forgetfulness of self that a gaze rests on us. Should I return the gaze openly? No, it was too dangerous to gamble on that defense. So, as though by chance, I had to scan the horizon in order for an instant to graze the quiet woman who could be perceived like a shadow behind the reflecting window.

Otherwise nothing happened. The telephone did not even ring, something that I could count on in unusual situations. I had become dispensable, if not even superfluous. And to the extent that this feeling took possession of me, to that very extent did my longing for the unknown woman diminish. No one in this city of geometricians, architects, and merchants was as superfluous as I, so ridiculously superfluous and useless, and had I not felt the gaze of the woman from across the street on me, I would have dissolved, would have melted, patient and earnest, into the quiet. Wonderfully light, like a hovering vessel of pain, I sat on my hard chair as though I had already arrived on the other side. This condition, which I had never before felt so near and familiar, was like a blessing. And the condition had allies: boredom and waiting, soothing emptiness. Had the unknown woman now entered, she would not have noticed me.

While I was staring so detached into the distance, the door opened. I did not look up, did not turn around, did not move at all until the steps behind me came to a stop.

"Are you alone?" asked a voice that I knew all too well. In this situation it was an unpleasant voice because it took me for granted to a certain extent, did not take offense at my presence.

"Yes, I'm alone," I said.

"Then we should go eat," said Fat Peter. "I don't guess you did any shopping."

28

I don't remember ever having seen a person who could so effortlessly stuff so much food into himself as the one who now for almost three whole hours had been sitting opposite me. With two silver fasteners he had draped on his chest a linen napkin that caught everything that did not go into his mouth at the first pass of the fork and helped it back onto his plate, everything that at the second or third attempt disappeared into the circular crater of his face. Soon the tablecloth was covered with spots and remains of food that he now and then snipped with his finger onto the floor. Some effort was required to persuade the restaurateur to bring ever-new dishes because they had not been provided for in the sequence of the menu. And even when what was desired was set down in the correct consistency and seasoning in front of this extraordinary glutton, long-lasting discussions followed about the proper preparation of the foodstuffs.

Now it was the temperature of the food that left much to be desired; now the temperature of the dinnerware or the tableware whose icy coldness — in particular, the knives — was found at fault. In addition, the salad, served with hot potatoes, had to be bedded in a different oil before it was even admitted as a salad. The spaghetti was a touch too soft, the seafood too long rinsed and consequently no longer salty enough, the sage under the liver presumably not fresh, the potatoes too sweet, thus probably old, the pheasant not hung long enough — every dish was subjected to an exact examination in the presence of the restaurateur, the waiter, and the chef before and during consumption, and when one of this desperate trio was about to turn to other tasks in the overcrowded restaurant, he was shouted after rudely that he ought at least to finish the discussion. Then the three trotted around with sunken heads, while Fat Peter took a few minutes to slurp a copious amount of wine with such maddening noises that soon the whole restaurant looked over at us with simultaneous amazement and repulsion.

It was left to me to express a wordless apology with a perturbed expression, since the fat man had closed his swollen eyelids during his hissing wine tasting. He was totally oblivious — there was no other way to express it — while I, a frugal diner who ate quickly and speedily and without a napkin, endeavored to draw the man into a conversation concerning my presence in Florence.

"One thing at a time" was his reply, before he dedicated himself to a specialty of the house, fat sausages on puréed beans, which the restaurateur, in the unfortunate hope of this time garnering nothing but praise, paid for from his own pocket. There was no reason to doubt the quality of the fat sausages. They were actually so fat that I had enough with one bite and slid my portion onto the fat man's plate, but here, too, substantial misgivings were expressed that were silenced only by a choking seizure. Accompanied by pounding on his back, the red-faced diner was taken to the toilet, which was separated from the dining room by a simple door and meant for both the sexes and from which

146

the whole restaurant participated in the discharge in reverse of foods with an acoustic quality never heard before.

"Indescribably bad sausage," growled the paunchy man, who after quite a while appeared alive and well again, crossing through the dining room, "incredibly bad sausage in Florence, unbelievable." And finally he yelled in a manner so loud and unrestrained for grappa that I had to believe he had lost his reason and good manners once and for all.

The restaurateur hauled out the last possible item before the check and beaming with joy brought a bottle of *mille erbe*, a poisonous-green liquid in which a few lost blades of grass swayed gently. I poured myself a few drops and the man opposite me a small glassful, which he took elegantly with thick fingers, swung it briefly in my direction to signify a toast, and then drank down in one gulp. The stuff burned as schnapps usually burns only in South American novels. It tore my throat open, took my breath, and brought tears to my eyes.

Fat Peter, on the other hand, poured himself in all tranquillity a second and on the heels of that a third glass, as though this oily drink should free him of all apprehensions and unwarranted expectations about the food. Parallel to the decrease of liquid in the bottle was a decrease in the store of rhetoric at the disposal of the colossus, and after the fourth glass his mighty head fell with its stringy hair onto his bib, which glowed with all colors from the meal. At the same time a piping tone escaped his mouth at a high pitch, breaking off and then beginning again deeper, while he made faint and slobbery agitated motions. The meal, as far as I could judge the situation, was over.

I have to admit that I was deeply impressed by this performance, which gave me a presentiment of the strategist and producer of great events. It was up to me, so went the rules of this game, to take care of the check and with a special tip to persuade the waiter, despite the insults he had suffered, to help me drag the hulking man to the Borgo San Lorenzo. He did so under protest until we reached the door to the building, but he could not be persuaded to transport the load up the narrow stairway. He left that to me alone and withdrew with a curse. Toward midnight I had arranged the fat body on the bed, rubbed cologne on it, because he threatened to stop breathing, and draped it with a blanket, out from which his two mole-sized hands peeped.

A woman had not been mentioned in our laconic table talk.

I was about to sit down at the window with the poet's Dante, in the hope of still being able to read something in the light of the sign, when I noticed how the light in the room opposite was turned off and a shadow lingered unmoving in the window. "You are watching, at least," I whispered. "I can count on you."

> *Once through the winter long before me stood*
> *A bush with thorns, a wilding one and short,*
> *Where later roses burgeoned from its wood. . .*
> *And I saw fleet and in the right direction sport*
> *A ship aflying on the ocean's heave*
> *And sinking having hardly neared its port.*
> *From this the know-it-alls should not believe*

148

On seeing one man rob and one bestow
That here indeed they God's decree perceive
Since ONE will rise and ONE will stay below.

Yes, even from a withered branch a leaf can sprout — this
wise word of Dante, which he tells the arrogant pair, Donna
Berta and Ser Martino, as a warning against doubting the
ways of the Lord, I wanted to make my own. Come what
will, I thought to myself, it doesn't matter whether the difficulties are solved. Why had the poet made an ordinary
Heaven out of Dante's Paradiso, where it is really a matter
of truth that has its roots in God? Why not Paradiso?

And why *know-it-alls* and not Mutt and Jeff, or Dame
Bertha and Sir Martin as it was, perhaps merely for the sake
of rhyme, in the nineteenth-century translation? And did one
understand the last line, which in the nineteenth-century
translation had been interpreted very clearly: "For the one
yet may rise and the other fall"? — *"Chè quel può surgere,
e quel può cadere."* I was about to inquire of Gmelin, the
dependable savior in all cases of doubt, but a vile belch from
the direction of the bed caused me to abandon it. "For the
one yet may rise and the other fall," I said aloud to myself,
rolled the deeply snoring man a bit onto his side, and,
shivering with cold, took possession of a narrow strip on the
right edge of the bed. How can that be translated, I
wondered incessantly. The one can yet ascend, the other fall
nastily? I left the translation machine to its own devices, as
sleep conquered me soundly despite the cold.

29

A clear morning, a rare thing in Florence at this time of year. I had gotten up early, gone to Santa Croce and lighted a candle, then into the Baptistery to study the portals, and finally into a bakery, where I bought a few rolls for breakfast. All the beggars whom the light had lured from the gloomy, repellent stone buildings were taken care of; the poor box provided for. Machiavelli and Michelangelo greeted me. Actually, nothing could go wrong on such a day.

In front of the Baptistery I had again met Bob Nockham, an ex-soldier and later a CIA agent, who one day had dropped the whole thing and begun a study of literature in Rome. At the time, he was living in the American Academy, where he worked in the kitchen. I had rented a studio in one of the nearby buildings and was hosted daily by him. He was my savior, this man like a tree, with elmlike feet. Both of us were then in love with a Danish poet who had received a royal stipendium to complete the final version of a long poem, an epic poem, but in our opinion she was too pretty for poetry. Together we dissuaded her, only in the next moment to initiate separate attacks on her again in the hope of conquest. She was a platinum blonde. Everything about her was platinum blond — she looked like an albino. I had dealt the American the greatest blow, when the Danish poet sat as a model for me for a whole week. For a week she had posed for me in her infinite whiteness, while Bob had to work at the academy.

Some of the paintings that came into being at that time I sold in Hanover; I gave Bob a drawing that thoroughly disconcerted him because I had put myself into the picture. He became a professor in Chicago and was engaged in developing the logical foundation of a concept of God that was of little interest to me, if I understood his letters correctly. But what I certainly did not understand was the enthusiasm with which he worked on this problem, his really erotic mania to design a logical construct of God without bothering even a whit about the content of faith.

So now he had turned up in front of the Baptistery in Florence. We embraced again after eighteen years, and he started right off, without asking me the reasons for my presence in this city, talking about his God constructs. A woman, apparently his wife, was standing with a pinched face to one side behind him. I tried to find a lacuna in his argumentation to get away.

He had developed a kind of scale into which he could enter his ideas about God and, in all seriousness, was on the point of drawing this concept for me with a rock on the ground in a kind of diagram. I had no desire to get involved in the logical subtleties in connection with God that were thought up in today's Chicago, although I could have contributed something to the theme. Besides, I had to go to my Fat Peter on the Borgo. Bob accompanied me, talking to me about concepts, and when we finally were standing in front of my building, he asked me whether I had ever slept with the Danish poet.

152

"No," I said.

"Good," said Bob. "Now we can be real friends again." We embraced earnestly without saying a word, then with long strides he was already on his way to the Baptistery, where he had lost or forgotten his wife.

The musty staircase could not shock me after this hearty meeting, nor even the sight of the shabby lodgings now crisscrossed by a broad path of light. Like a fat king, the colossus was sitting in bed with the grimy napkin held by the silver fasteners still around his neck. By what understanding of the world did this man let himself be led, who with no reticence sat on the bed in his suit and shoes, his hair jutting away from his head in tangles, without a sense of guilt and without remorse? Shamelessly, yes, shamelessly he was sitting there among the crumpled pillows.

"Coffee?" was his first question.

"Croissants?" My own followed directly afterward.

"The first cup black with lots of sugar," he called after me, "the second with hot milk."

I did as I was told and brought the whole breakfast obediently to our common bed. He ate and drank. I was silent because, after all, I knew that at this work — and for him it was work, even though robbed of a sense of importance — he could not be disturbed. But the time came when I had to ask questions.

"Where is she and when is she coming?" I asked, and was ashamed to have struck such an inquisitorial tone.

"Who?" he asked back.

"I was ordered to come here to this apartment," I said uncertainly, because the fat king was looking at me as curiously with his inquisitive sea-lion face as though I had spoken about a logical proof of God. "I have to get back to my easel as you can imagine, to my Dante. I can't possibly fritter away my days here in idleness, you can understand that."

"I'm not keeping you," said the king, "for all I care, you can go. Besides, the bed is too narrow for two — and, in the end, two people under one sheet don't always have the same dream."

"But surely you know when she's coming?" I asked. "If she's coming?"

I wasn't certain whether it was a bad comedy or a good joke that I was witnessing, for the fat man kept looking ahead droopily with a wrinkled brow, let his fat lower lip hang down, and with his little finger scratched behind his ear like a cat.

"Who's Dante?" he said.

"When is the woman coming?" I asked.

"The devil knows what woman you mean," he said.

"The one who stole my Duck," I said.

Sadly he looked at me with little red eyes, almost in desperation.

"Dante, Duck," he mumbled at a loss.

"With whom you assaulted a French policeman," I said on an off chance.

He got up, stretched his immense body, walked to the window. I looked after him and over his shoulder looked at the window on the other side of the street, where silent and gray the woman was at her post. He waved across, the woman waved a gaunt hand back. He bowed a bit, with accomplished courtesy.

"Sits there year in and year out, wondering what kind of crooks find a hideout here," he said.

"The one you were in France with," I said, "in Grazimis."

"Oh," he said, "nothing came of that, had no sense for the market and trade. Wanted to get involved deep or not at all. And always on the level of dollars. Not anything for me, I told her, and did so loud and clear."

"And when is she coming to Florence?"

"The devil knows," he said "I can ask, if you'll have the goodness to give me the phone."

He lay down on the bed again, sighing heavily. There followed a long conversation in Italian, the content of which I understood little enough. There was talk of dollars, the weather, people, but I was in the dark about what kind of relationship they had with one another. My bed partner seemed to telephone with great pleasure. He actually sucked at the receiver, laughed, cursed, snorted, scratched his immense belly, and at short intervals broke wind that he fanned away with his free hand.

Then this interlude, too, was at an end. The receiver was replaced on the hook. The colossus climbed leg by leg out of bed, smoothed his suit, finally got rid of the napkin, smoothed his hair down flat on his skull, and made all kinds of other arrangements without saying a word to me. An actor, I thought, a comedian who knows exactly when his next line must come, with a sense for timing, a feel for the right tempo.

"Natalia will come and give you a report," he said finally, with that courtesy that occasionally characterizes fat people.

With these words he picked up the little satchel that he had put down the day before, waved in my direction, and prepared to take off. "I'd advise you," he said at the door, "not to draw any attention to yourself leaving or entering the apartment. And maybe it would also be possible for you to forgo any female visitors during your stay here, if you know what I mean."

I hurried to the window to get one more glance at him and to reassure myself that he had really left the apartment, and I saw him already on the street, his right hand raised for a gracious wave, first in my direction, then in the direction of the old lady in the window opposite, who, charmed, answered the wave.

30

From the window, against which I had leaned, my right foot on the low windowsill, my hands folded over my knee, I looked down onto the Borgo, which was now thronged. What elegance of motion, as though none of the people below had ever done any work. A ballet of bows, of quick embraces, of hidden greetings, a well-ordered system of signals that was recognizable as structured only from above. Everyone obeyed the rules of the game, even the loner who, with an unfriendly expression, crossed the lines of people and in so doing drew glances, whereby new constellations resulted immediately. A prism.

For a long time I kept my eyes locked on a couple trying to say farewell with every means at their disposal. At first I took this scene, too, for a piece out of a repertoire, perfect and coordinated, because every movement was right, but the more my gaze fixed on the two people and isolated them, detached them from the surrounding structure, the more they, for their part, shed the structure that laid its play of form all around them. Now the woman stood with staring eyes, arms dangling, in front of the bakery. Her shoulder bag, slipped from her arm, gently touched the ground. Her right foot was in front of her left one, as though she were about to run after the departing man, but her torso was contrarily bent slightly backward. The man, only a few yards away, turned around once more, perhaps to wave, saw the woman in her comically twisted posture, turned back immediately, and took her in his arms again, whereupon they could not decide over which shoulder they should lay their heads. They stood there as though welded together, like a statue by Brancusi, man and woman out of one stone.

Now they broke apart to an extent, held hands with one another, looking into one another's eyes. A drama, a rare tragedy. Did she have to go to an office, he to the university? Would they see one another again in a few hours, eat together, go to the movies? Now he pushed her gently away, to make her departure easier, but she held his hands so tightly in her own that only a slight swaying arose, no real parting. Distracted by a musician who with his violin walked through the multitude, I had missed the moment of the actual farewell, and my eyes, accustomed to the couple, almost overlooked the woman now alone again, standing in front of the bakery in a pleading attitude. But the young man was still there, only a few yards away in front of a shoe store, his face turned toward her. So they stood facing one another, at a distance, and tested their mutual powers of attraction, and everything looked as if they would fall into one another's arms again immediately.

But now the man took a step backward, a single step, that sufficed to release him from the enchanted circle: he turned around and left, without once more turning his head, in the direction of San Lorenzo. The woman lingered in a waiting attitude, with wide-open eyes, as though she were rooted to the spot. She evidently could not grasp that the man had left, for even now she shook her head with its abundant mane a bit. So she stood there, the immovable particle in a system in motion.

In the fifteenth century the *leggi suntuane* were enacted in Florence to check the dissipation of its citizens. Embossed satin with a silken background was allowed to be worn only by small numbers, as were the brocades from the Orient, woven from silver and gold threads. In a bookstore next to Santa Croce I had bought the sermons of Bernardino of Siena, who also had given the Florentines a good dressing-down. In vain.

> *How shall I describe the luxury that we meet not only in the palaces of the great but likewise in the houses of common citizens? Just consider how broad and soft the beds are. There you will find bedclothes of silk and linen with gold embroidery, splendidly painted coverlets that excite the desires of the senses, and in addition gilded, painted bed curtains. If one were to take such a garment and were to squeeze it and wring it, then one would be able to see the blood of living human beings well forth.*

I was prevented from imagining the reflections of Bernardino further by the entrance of Natalia.

She said, "We can leave."

I packed my books together. Natalia filled my culture satchel and stuffed it in my traveling bag, as though we had long ago prepared for this departure together.

I waved gratefully to the woman at the window, who with a quick movement at once turned her head away; took my bag, and followed Natalia down the stairs and to her car, a small Alfa Romeo with a Swiss license plate, which was parked in front of San Lorenzo, that untidy shed.

We drove back and forth through the city as though through a maze. Behind Santa Maria del Carmine we found a parking place and went on foot to my dentist, who put in a splendid new tooth. He was enthusiastic about his work, even called Natalia, whom he naturally knew personally, into the treatment room to attest to his work and praise it.

I was taken care of.

We left Florence in a southeast direction, if I had calculated the place of the sun correctly, and, beyond a village with the name of Incisa, left the highway for a hilly region that affected me so directly that I asked the silent driver of the car to make a short stop: I wanted to draw. Without quibbling, she agreed at once and climbed up a small rise with me from which I had the best view over the terraced fields.

"Where are we driving to?" I asked.

"We're more or less there," she said, and sat down a few yards away on a boulder so that, in view of the expanse that surrounded us, I had a firm point for my work. "In the beginning, when my imagination began to rove in madness, certain faces of women appeared to me with disheveled hair, who said: 'You, too, will die,' and then, after the women, more faces appeared to me, rare and horrible to see, who said to me: 'You are dead.' When my imagination began to rove so much in madness, I got to the point where I no longer knew where I was; and it seemed to me that I saw weeping women walking along the path, with disheveled hair and unspeakably sad; and it was as though I saw the sun turn dark and as though the birds in flight fell dead onto the earth."

I made four drawings, a small series, that depicted birds fallen from the sky, next to a woman who, with her back to the observer, her head propped on her hand, stares at the dead creatures.

"You're going to catch cold," said Natalia. "We ought to drive on."

We drove up and down through vineyards and stands of woods, and in less than ten minutes we stopped at a small farm that was populated by all kinds of feathered fowl, cats, a donkey, and a barking dog. I saw no people.

"I'll show you your room," said Natalia.

The casual nature of this sentence and the indifference with which it was spoken could not be reconciled with my expectations, which were still directed to a meeting with the unknown woman, nor did they promote my readiness to take part much longer in this game.

"To whom does this farm belong?" I asked.

"Hans and Beatrice," was the answer, "but that's not important."

Beatrice? I had to laugh at the idea that the woman I sought, the one with the long nose, should share the very same name with the one who looks transfigured into the face of the one *qui est per omnia secula benedictus*.

"Is Beatrice at home?" I asked.

"How do I know?" said Natalia.

I followed my escort, as though I were attached to her, through the kitchen and the vestibule on the second floor, where she led me into a room in which there were two beds, a table in front of the window framing the landscape, two chairs, and a huge wardrobe.

"Which bed do you want?" she asked me.

I pointed to the one from which I could look out the window, whereupon she stretched out on the other.

31

For three whole days I sketched in that landscape. Occasionally I took the donkey along, which followed me willingly and thus appeared with its melancholy ears on many a sheet. Sometimes I took the dog. In the evening I met a group of six or seven people in the roomy kitchen, where there was risotto with mushrooms. Afterward, I translated a bit in my room, even though listlessly, because the conspicuous presence of Natalia irritated me. I didn't say a word to her.

Once, in my bad Italian, I asked one of the farmers I met in the fields where Florence might lie, but the thought of wandering alone through the hilly landscape to the city caused me to drop the idea at once. The man had made a gesture that more or less encompassed the whole panorama, wherever you go, he meant, lies Florence.

So the short days passed, and the sketch pads filled with curiously allegorical things when it was raining outside, with abstract-universal landscapes on clear days.

I drew the lion as the symbol of arrogance, the leopard as vanity, and the she-wolf as avarice; I sketched two skeletons that embraced through eternity, draped with thin, wafting veils. I felt my strengths and my weaknesses profoundly — the ability to isolate the individual object, but also the wretched inclination to imprint the heightened depiction of my own problems to the utmost depths onto every sheet. The deeper I penetrated the graphic execution of Paradise, the more invisible my opponent became. And since I made no sort of effort to get to the secret of the house and its idle residents, they soon saw in me a kind of sketching house pet that needed its repose and left them in peace.

On the second of December, my mother's birthday, I took a long walk into the mountains, with the dog as my companion. That is, actually he was my leader. I followed him as far as the flat stone walls forming the boundary of the fields and olive groves allowed. I felt free and could stride forward unimpeded, unburdened by any torments in my mind. In the same measure that the memory of the woman without a name faded, my peace increased, and I even began to sing out loud so that the land all around could have a share in my joy.

We had been under way a good two hours when the dog turned into a cypress lane that led to a farm hidden behind some trees. I tried in vain to whistle him back, indeed, the louder I called, the more resolutely he followed his nose, until I followed him unwillingly. The path was paved with gravel, between which moist moss emerged; there was a smell of decay and ashes.

Soon I was standing in front of a crumbling, pale red country house from whose chimney thin smoke climbed into the air. Ivy grew up the stone walls on trellises and framed the windows, all of which were tightly locked by shutters. The dog cowered whimpering in front of the house door under a projecting arbor and could not be coaxed to leave the strange property. When I started to pull him away by his collar, speaking to him good-humoredly, he snapped at my hand.

"You want some water," I said to him. "Come along into the shed, there's bound to be a faucet there." We were busy figuring out a compromise when the door opened and a man appeared in the doorway. The dog immediately leapt upon him with joy and he responded to this sign of recognition.

"There you are," he said to me. "I was getting afraid that you were lost. In wintertime the landscape is almost indecisive about which of its paths it should offer, the ones into the heart or the ones into pain."

In the bluish-tinged kitchen was a splendid wooden table set for two, and in the twinkling of an eye a bowl of steaming spaghetti was sitting before me, next to it a carafe of red wine. The dog, too, had his food before him.

The man spoke with a Hungarian accent about Germany, which he obviously had once loved but now followed with distrust, and he wanted to know from me whether the rich store of prejudices that he ostensibly had at his disposal could be increased even more.

"A masterfully unsuccessful creation," I said, even though I could not stand conversations of this sort about that subject. "You need have no fear. A merciless petite bourgeoisie, which became wealthy on both sides of an impossible border, that wants to and will unite by any means, even disgraceful ones. And good banks, good money. But under that glittering coat beats a sentimental heart that you have to watch out for."

This information seemed to relieve him. He smiled to

himself, made a few awkward attempts to get the conversation going again by murmuring something about a world-state and about world-state controls, about the age of total power politics and about the sovereign who with his breath would once again set the ashes of our hopes to dancing, but he was discouraged by my stubborn silence from putting the confused threads of his high-flown but not exactly original views into a firm framework.

"I like you," he said suddenly, without warning, as though I were for sale. "You prefer the broad brush, not pointillist coloration."

I felt uncomfortable and thus not in a position to divert this thin flow of fateful chatter into the direction in which my interests lay.

"Are you often at the other farm?" I asked. "I've never seen you there."

"No," he said, "those people reject me. They always want to change, be someone else, like the gods, that's the frightful thing. It feeds on their capital, empties it. Instead of sorting out their holdings and keeping them, they devour them by constant transformation. Their capital was long ago swallowed up, leaving them with anxiety!"

To find a stopping place in this tangle was hopeless, so I gave it up. "May I use your phone?" I asked him. "Make a long-distance call?"

Wearily he got up and led me to an adjacent room that was full of old tapestries on which ancient mythology celebrated its festivals.

"Here," he said, and handed me the receiver, "maybe

you'll have better luck than I. I've been trying to reach her by phone for two weeks and have always missed her."

I was so stunned by what I heard that I had to give myself a shake to snap into my old composure, but then I took the receiver with my trembling hand and, when the somber fellow had left the room, dialed Monsieur Jopin's number in Grazimis.

"Where are you?" he said gruffly, when I had finally made myself comprehensible. "Police everywhere. Excitement, disquiet. The tower burned down, as you surely know already. Better that you don't ever come back, so that we'll have peace and quiet."

32

The police had taken what the fire had spared or only touched slightly to the police station and recorded it properly, altogether about two hundred pieces that were stored in a bad-smelling room. Most of the things that I had to identify with an official were cracked in two, split to pieces, and charred, but the paintings, in spite of their easy flammability, in spite of the oil paints and wooden frames, were almost untouched and merely covered with a veil of soot that even lent them an additional, eerie expressiveness, driven and somewhat darkly smudged, that matched the autumnal motifs and pleased me greatly. They had survived the trial by fire. Not spontaneous joy, not intellectual reflections, and not an exertion of will had transformed them, rather something else. But what? The fire, only the fire? In any case they were no longer my paintings.

The policeman was obviously of another opinion concerning the quality of the canvases, for he stated without regret that I could consign the whole pile of trash to the dump, and he offered to get started right away. I gave him the articles of clothing and a part of the tubes of pigment that had melted together from the heat, my big wooden paint box, a present from my second wife, tied to all kinds of memories but now half burned up, my pocket watch, the radio, and all the records, which he obediently threw into the trash can, while noting this on his list.

After long questioning by the inspector, enlightened about the state of the investigation, they let me call a moving company that was to take care of the rest: fourteen large and six small canvases, eighteen sketch pads, a few brushes, scrapers, rulers, odds and ends. And finally, miraculously, the entire Dante library had been rescued, around a hundred works, some of them valuable — the rare Italian editions, the Dante yearbooks, and even the first editions of translations by the poet and by another twentieth-century translator, as well as all my handwritten research notes.

A miracle, better to leave it alone.

The detective had informed me that Monsieur Jopin's daughter was to be thanked for the discovery of the fire. She had rescued what the police had so carefully listed; she had called the fire department and informed the police.

I should be grateful to her, he had said, even if gratitude wasn't among my preferred virtues.

"And did she set the house on fire?" I asked. "To be able to rescue the paintings?"

He looked at me as though he wanted to put a curse on me, but no words issued from his mouth, only hissing sounds. Somehow or other he had given up wanting to educate a German criminal to whom not even the honor of thieves was sacred.

This time I had to agree to stay in town, for which reason I requested the detective to get a room for me in a hotel on the outskirts. From there I called the German art historian in Florence and asked her to leave a note in the Borgo San Lorenzo with the information that Natalia's Alfa

Romeo, which I had taken after returning from my Hungarian host, had been dropped off at the Hertz parking place in Milan and the keys had been left at the counter, which she promised to do if I would give her my address in France.

I gave her the tower telephone number, there she could talk to the swallows and the bats.

With that I had done everything that was to be done.

It was three days before Christmas. The light was strangely tremulous, and the horizon had something profoundly dirty about it. I walked to the tower, along the river, whose brackish water exuded a bitter smell. The door had been burned up and replaced by barbed wire; fragments of china and scraps of cloth lay everywhere. From the ivy-covered oak, from which the branches on the house side had been cut and which now looked like an unfinished sculpture, the water dripped bright and bubbly into a puddle that seemed not to drain. A strong east wind blew over the hill, and so I forced my way under the barbed wire into the kitchen. Table and chairs lay as if tossed together in one of the corners, which was strewn with shards. The blue plastic bucket was sitting in the sink. The water on the floor had mixed with the pigments and taken on a greenish black color. Over everything hung a repulsive stench.

I squatted on my heels to be able to absorb this picture in peace. What had happened? With this mad deed, with this act of an insane person, had a sign been given? Had the true sense of my life's endeavors, accomplished with great effort, to capture the last corner of nature in paintings far away from people and their activities, been opened to question by this flaming sign, and should the reading of Dante, equally holding off the world, be interrupted by a flare of fire without my having been allowed to feel the comfort and the peace that I expected from this pursuit?

But who was giving the signs here? Did they come from me, or did I attract them, which came to the same thing? Did I want to interrupt myself, stay my hand?

I was making such an effort with these questions, so carefully intent on not slipping into self-pity that I was unaware of the cold, which with biting strength had taken hold of me and made me hunch in my crouching, cowering position as though frozen fast. Finally, enervated by physical weakness, I suddenly fell over, just toppled sideways into the iridescent mire, which my sweater greedily absorbed.

I cursed, complained, and cried out as though I had lost my mind, sneered at the unreasonable demands of the region and its inhabitants, at the decay that had fallen on everyone and everything, the stifling terror. With my foot I kicked the residue of everything that had at first made my sojourn so enjoyable, and, shaken by fear and fury, I raged, insanely gesticulating all around, my face contorted, as though I were a prisoner for life in this tower and not a free man who could leave it forthwith.

In the door stood Monsieur Jopin's daughter, mute, motionless, staring.

"What are you doing here?" I asked her, but received no answer. She was standing there strangely stiff, her feet side by side in perfect symmetry, her hands in the pockets of her anorak, staring at me with a gaze in which nothing could be

172

read. "I want to hear something," I said, "objections, excuses, explanations. You can't stand around here so pitifully without a word. Say something," I pleaded, when she still gave no sign of opening her mouth, "say a sentence, a word, a syllable. Don't drive me insane with your muteness."

Since she did not move, I sprang toward her, grabbed her and shook her, and finally slapped her face.

She pushed out her lower lip and let an almost soundless murmur be heard, but remained standing like a statue under the tragically bent door beam, encapsulated in a muteness that was not to be forced open by anything in the world.

Then I took her in my arms, laid her head on my dirty pullover, and caressed her back until incessantly and steadily my own tears came, only the precursors of a continuous, world-devouring sobbing.

33

On Christmas Eve I was permitted to leave Grazimis. Whether for humanitarian reasons or because they expected no further explanation from me could not be determined. I promised the detective to write down a detailed report from my perspective, which he would put in the files, and additionally I had to leave behind a German address. "We'll clear up the case," he called out to me at my departure, as I was setting off for the train station. The wind was blowing smacking cold blasts over the marketplace, pressing my clothing tightly to my body. "We'll meet again."

In the train to Toulouse, which traveled jolting through the bare landscape, I tried to compose myself with Dante and kept reading until I had to lay the book aside, affected:

> *From the highest sky which rolls the thunder down*
> *No mortal eye is stationed so remote,*
> *Though in the deepest of the seas it drown,*
> *As then from Beatrice was my sight; but naught*
> *It was to me; for without any veil*
> *Her image down to me undimmed was brought.*

There they were, sitting around me, the strange shapes that impudently and stubbornly had taken possession of my life. I needed only to draw them. Despite the dim light and the rhythmic jerks of the train, I soon had them on paper, tiny persons in an empty space, all that was missing was language to get them talking.

"Speak," I whispered with bent head over the paper, "show me the threads that bind you, so that I will understand! Don't run through my life as though over fresh fields, don't leave tracks behind that stop somewhere! Every human being has the right to a story with a beginning and an end, every human being should know who possesses him. Don't keep changing your appearances and your habits, otherwise you'll be nothing, sand, wind, dots on a white sheet of paper."

When the train entered Toulouse, I had in my hand a black-covered piece of paper that showed a white fleck only at the top left. I pulled down the window and gave it to the wind, which took it and swallowed it up with an ugly hiss.

It was time to begin a new painting.

For Ludger Geerdes

176